MAROONED WITH BURMA

COPYRIGHT 1986 NBM PUBLISHING
COVER BY RAY FEHRENBACH
ISBN# 0-918348-23-4

Terry & The Pirates is a registered
trademark of Tribune Media Services, Inc.

THE FLYING BUTTRESS CLASSICS LIBRARY is an imprint of:

NANTIER·BEALL·MINOUSTCHINE
Publishing co.
new york

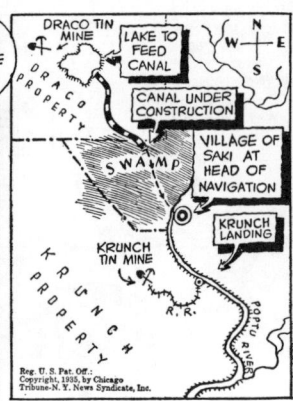

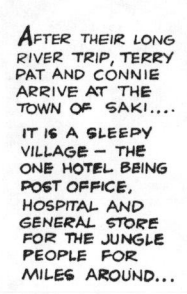

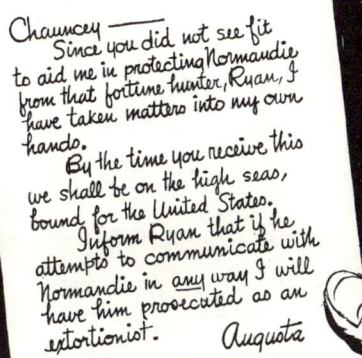

ALL HERE, BUT THE BOATMAN! - WHERE'S HE?
I SAW HIM DRIFTIN' AWAY ON A PACKIN' CASE! - HE'S NOT DROWNED!
12-25
HEY, ON DECK - HAUL US UP, WILL YOU?
NO ANSWER! WHERE'S TH' CREW O' THIS TUB ANYHOW?
WE'LL HAVE TO CLIMB IT, LADS! - COME ON!
MILTON CANIFF
Reg. U. S. Pat. Off.; Copyright, 1935, by Chicago Tribune-N. Y. News Syndicate, Inc.
NOT A SOUL IN SIGHT! THIS IS DARN QUEER!
OOOH - IS SPOOK SHIP! -MEBBE GOT CREW OF GHOSTS! -IS SCARY SCOW!

TALK ABOUT HIT AN' RUN DRIVERS! THIS SHIP WRECKS US - AND NO ONE EVEN HELPS US UP ON DECK!
SPOOK SHIP! - THA'S WHAT 'TIS!
12-26
BOATS JUS' DON'T GO SCOOTIN' AROUN' ALL BY THEMSELVES!
Reg. U. S. Pat. Off.; Copyright, 1935, by Chicago Tribune-N. Y. News Syndicate, Inc.
WE'LL LOOK ON TH' BRIDGE - THERE'S BOUND TO BE SOMEBODY STEERING!
MEBBE SHIP GOT OUTRAGEOUS DISEASE AN' SAILORS ALL GO ELSEWAYS!!
HELLO! YOU HAVE COMPANY! - WHERE'S YOUR SENSE OF HOSPITALITY? - STILL NO ANSWER!
PAT! LOOK!
MILTON CANIFF

WHAT'S TH' MATTER, TERRY?
LOOK! -JIST LOOK!
OOH - F' HEAVEN'S - F' PETE'S F' GOO'NESS - WHIZ!
12-27
MILTON CANIFF
SAY, MISTER - YOUR SHIP RAN US DOWN! - WE WANT TO GET TO THE COAST! YOU'RE HEADED DOWN STREAM! - GUESS WE'LL HAVE TO RIDE ALONG!
Reg. U. S. Pat. Off.; Copyright, 1935, by Chicago Tribune-N. Y. News Syndicate, Inc.
YOU JUMP OVERSIDE! -SWIM AWAY QUICK! GO!

WHAT DO YOU MEAN, JUMP OVERBOARD? - WITH THAT TIDE RUNNING A MAN COULDN'T LIVE!
OVERSIDE! - GO SUDDEN, OR I SHOOT!
12-28
AT LEAST GIVE US A BOAT! - WE DON'T WANT TO DROWN!
NO BOAT! - SWIM OR DROWN - NO DIFFERENCE TO ME!
MILTON CANIFF
Reg. U. S. Pat. Off.; Copyright, 1935, by Chicago Tribune-N. Y. News Syndicate, Inc.
- LOOKS AS IF WE'LL HAVE TO HIT TH' DRINK, FELLAHS - BUT-
- NOT RIGHT NOW!

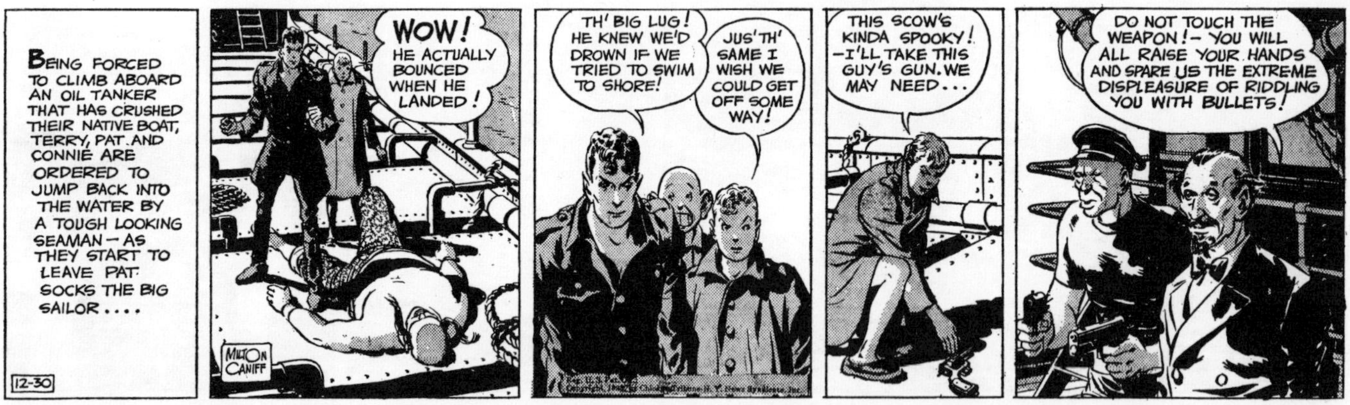
BEING FORCED TO CLIMB ABOARD AN OIL TANKER THAT HAS CRUSHED THEIR NATIVE BOAT, TERRY, PAT AND CONNIE ARE ORDERED TO JUMP BACK INTO THE WATER BY A TOUGH LOOKING SEAMAN — AS THEY START TO LEAVE PAT SOCKS THE BIG SAILOR....
12-30
MILTON CANIFF
WOW! HE ACTUALLY BOUNCED WHEN HE LANDED!
TH' BIG LUG! HE KNEW WE'D DROWN IF WE TRIED TO SWIM TO SHORE!
JUS' TH' SAME I WISH WE COULD GET OFF SOME WAY!
THIS SCOW'S KINDA SPOOKY! -I'LL TAKE THIS GUY'S GUN. WE MAY NEED...
DO NOT TOUCH THE WEAPON! - YOU WILL ALL RAISE YOUR HANDS AND SPARE US THE EXTREME DISPLEASURE OF RIDDLING YOU WITH BULLETS!

WHAT IS THIS? WHO ARE YOU? WHAT'S IT ALL ABOUT?
A PERFECTLY LOGICAL QUESTION, MY GOOD MAN!
12-31
UNFORTUNATELY I AM NOT AT LIBERTY TO ANSWER YOU!
YOU MIGHT TELL US WHY THIS BIG GUY TRIED TO MAKE US SWIM TO SHORE...
HE MERELY OBEYED ORDERS IN A MANNER TYPICAL OF HIS LOW MENTAL STATURE!
Reg. U. S. Pat. Off.: Copyright, 1935, by Chicago Tribune-N. Y. News Syndicate, Inc.
NANCHIK! CONDUCT THESE GENTLEMEN TO THE BRIG! - I SHALL SPEAK TO THEM AT MY LEISURE!
GO!
OH WOE — AS ALWAYS! PICKLEMENTS BY TH' PECK! FUTURE IS MOST UNROSY!
MILTON CANIFF

WHAT'S TH' BIG IDEA! — WE'VE DONE NOTHING TO YOU! WHY DON'T YOU PUT US ASHORE?
IT WOULD BE WISE TO SAVE THE HEROICS FOR A MORE OPPORTUNE OCCASION!
1-1
WHY YOU SMIRKING LITTLE RUNT I'LL BUST...
HOLD IT, PAT! — WE'D JUS' GET SHOT UP! HE'S GOT US IN A SPOT!
GO INSIDE SUDDEN!
WHAT A FINE DUMP THIS IS!
VELLY UNHAPPY ODOR IS PRESENT!
MILTON CANIFF
WELL, GENTLEMEN — I HOPE YOU LIKE THE CABIN I'VE ENGAGED FOR OUR 'ROUND THE WORLD CRUISE! — THE BREAD AND WATER IS EXCELLENT TOO, THE TELL ME!
I HOPE THEY FURNISH SADDLES FOR THE RATS! — WE COULD GET SOME EXERCISE!
Reg. U. S. Pat. Off.: Copyright, 1936, by Chicago Tribune-N. Y. News Syndicate, Inc.

TALK ABOUT HIT AN' RUN DRIVERS! -WE GET SMACKED BY A TANKER—THEN TOSSED IN THE BRIG! IT DOESN'T MAKE SENSE!
WHAT'S IT ALL ABOUT? -THAT CAPTAIN TALKS LIKE A COLLEGE PROF!
1-2
- BUT HE ACTS LIKE A BANDIT! - IN ALL THIS WORLD - WE WOULD RUN INTO THIS SHIP
MAYHAP WE IS SHANGHAIED! -YOU KNOW- BUMP FELLERS ON NOODLE T' GIT CREW!
— POSSIBLY — BUT I THINK IT'S WORSE THAN THAT! THIS SMOOTH TALKIN' CAPTAIN IS NO ORDINARY SKIPPER!
THIS SUSPENSE IS GETTIN' ME!.. -WISH WE COULD DO SOMETHIN'!
Reg. U. S. Pat. Off.: Copyright, 1936, by Chicago Tribune-N. Y. News Syndicate, Inc.
CONNIE TOO! -WOULD BE FUN TO SEE GOOD EXCITIN' GANGSTER MOOM PITCHER!
MILTON CANIFF

PAT—WHY D'YA S'PPOSE TH' CAPTAIN TOSSED US IN TH' BRIG?—YOU'D THINK WE WUZ PIRATES!
Y'GOT ME, PAL! —HE'S A MIGHTY SLICK DUCK TO BE SKIPPER OF AN OIL TANKER!
1-3
OOH!—MAYHAP SHIP IS FULL OF CASTOR OIL WHICH WICKED OL' CAPTAIN MAKE US DLINK!
WHAT I LIKE ABOUT YOU, CONNIE, IS THE NICE CHEERFUL THINGS YOU SAY!
SSHH! TH' DOORS OPENIN'!
Reg. U. S. Pat. Off., Copyright, 1936, by Chicago Tribune-N. Y. News Syndicate, Inc.
MASTER SAY YOU COME TO HIS CABIN! —SUDDEN!
BRUSH OFF YOUR TOP HATS, LADS! —WE HAVE AN AUDIENCE WITH HIS HIGHNESS!
MILTON CANIFF

YOU ARE DOUBTLESS WONDERING WHY I HAD YOU THROWN IN THE BRIG..
OH, NOT AT ALL! -THE PLACE WAS SO LUXURIOUS WE NEVER GAVE IT A THOUGHT!
1-4
Reg. U. S. Pat. Off. Copyright, 1936, by Chicago Tribune-N. Y. News Syndicate, Inc.
YOU'LL REGRET THAT FLIPPANCY, YOUNG MAN!
ALL RIGHT! OUT WITH IT!—WHAT'S TH' BIG IDEA!
MASTER! FRENCH PATROL BOAT ALONGSIDE! —ALREADY OFFICER ON DECK!
THOSE BLUNDERING FOOLS!
MILTON CANIFF
I HAVE A GUN UNDER THIS TABLE—I WILL TELL THE OFFICER I CANNOT STAND UP BECAUSE OF A SPRAINED ANKLE!—ONE WORD FROM YOU AND I SHOOT YOU ALL!

TERRY, PAT AND CONNIE ARE HELD PRISONER ON AN OIL TANKER BY A STRANGE LITTLE MAN....
THEY HAVE JUST BEEN ORDERED TO HIS CABIN WHEN A FRENCH HARBOR PATROL BOAT DRAWS ALONGSIDE AND AN OFFICER CLIMBS ABOARD...
1-6
TOO LATE FOR YOU TO LEAVE—! ONE WORD TO THIS OFFICER, AND I SHOOT YOU DOWN WITH THIS GUN I HAVE UNDER THE TABLE!
MASTER IN HERE!
M'SIEU LE CAPITAN! —I AM REGRET I MUS' ASK TO SEE YOUR PAPAIRS!
OF COURSE!
MILTON CANIFF
SO SORRY I MUST REMAIN SEATED! I TWISTED MY ANKLE RECENTLY! —VERY PAINFUL!
AH! C'EST DOMAGE! —NOW THE PAPAIRS, IF YOU PLEASE, M'SIEU!
THERE MUST BE SOME WAY TO OUT-SMART THIS GUY!—GOT TO THINK FAST...
Reg. U. S. Pat. Off., Copyright, 1936, by Chicago Tribune-N. Y. News Syndicate, Inc.

HERE ARE MY SAILING PAPERS, SIR! JUST A PLAIN OIL TANKER, UNITED STATES CHARTER. PLYING BETWEEN SINGAPORE AND SHANGHAI WITH OIL FOR THE MASTADON COMPANY OF NEW YORK!
1-7
SO!— EVERYTHING SEEMS IN ORDAIR!
THANK YOU! —BY THE WAY, WHY ALL THIS VIGILANCE BY THE FRENCH NAVY?
Reg. U. S. Pat. Off., Copyright, 1936, by Chicago Tribune-N. Y. News Syndicate, Inc.
AH, M'SIEU! —I AM NOT AT LEEBAIRTY TO SAY!—I MUS' BEED YOU BON SOIR!
GOTTA MAKE A BREAK BEFORE HE LEAVES!—IF I CAN JUST GET BEHIND HIM WITHOUT.....
MILTON CANIFF

AS PAT MOVES TO GET THE FRENCH OFFICER BETWEEN HIM AND THE SKIPPER'S CONCEALED GUN, HE IS STRUCK ON THE HEAD
1-8
PAT!
WHAT EE-S THEES!
MY WORD!
AH-ER! ONE OF MY CREW-UP FOR BEING DRUNK!-EVIDENTLY JUST PASSED OUT!
AH, SO! -I GO NOW!- AU REVOIR!
Reg. U. S. Pat. Off.: Copyright, 1936, by Chicago Tribune-N. Y. News Syndicate, Inc.
NO! NO! -HELP MIST--- BLUB!
MILTON CANIFF

YOU'VE HURT MY PAL!- -WE NEVER DID ANYTHIN' TO YOU! PAT! PAT!
EVIL OL' MAN! BETCHA GOBLINS GITCHA! -PULL OUT WHISKERS ONE AT TIME!
1-9
SILENCE! -YOUR FRIEND WAS ATTEMPTING SOME FOOLISH HEROICS!-HE GOT WHAT HE DESERVED!
HOW YOU LIKE, MASTER? -I SMASHUM BIG ONE WITH GUN!
VERY OPPORTUNE! THROW HIM IN THE BOILER ROOM! WHEN HE COMES TO HAVE THE CHIEF ENGINEER PUT HIM TO WORK!
SO, MASTER! -WILL DO!
THAT'S SHANGHAIING! YOU CAN'T DO IT! IT'S AGAINST TH' LAW!
-AH, MY OUTSPOKEN YOUNG MAN! YOU FORGET THAT I AM THE LAW HERE!
MILTON CANIFF
Reg. U. S. Pat. Off.: Copyright, 1936, by Chicago Tribune-N. Y. News Syndicate, Inc.

YOU MAY BE SKIPPER O' THIS SHIP - BUT YOU'VE SHANGHAIED US, AN' YOU BETTER LET US GO.- OR, OR--
OR WHAT?
1-10
WE ARE NOW ON THE OPEN SEA!- PERHAPS YOU'D LIKE TO SWIM ASHORE AND RUN TO THE POLICE..
OR, IF THAT WOULD TIRE YOU, NO DOUBT YOU HAVE A CARRIER PIGEON WHICH YOU WILL RELEASE TO BRING HELP...
GWAN! -RUB IT IN 'CAUSE YOU'VE GOT US IN A SPOT!
Reg. U. S. Pat. Off.: Copyright, 1936, by Chicago Tribune-N. Y. News Syndicate, Inc.
-SO! YOU APPRECIATE MY SARCASM! THEN YOU ARE WISE ENOUGH TO KEEP QUIET AND TAKE ORDERS- AND YOU WILL NOT BE HURT! GO BELOW!
MIST' TERRY, I GOTTA FEELIN' WE GONNA DO LIKE HE SAY!
MILTON CANIFF

YOU SLEEP THIS PLACE! -MAKE TROUBLE -GET SMASH ON FACE!
GO 'WAY OL' EVIL SON OF STUPID TADPOLE!
1-11
PAT'S HURT!-AN' WE'RE LOCKED UP ON AN OIL TANKER BY A GUY WHO MUST BE UP TO SOME MONKEY BUSINESS!
IN SOUP TO EYEBROWS! -VELLY UNHOTSY DANDY!
NO USE KIDDIN' OURSELVES!- THEY'VE GOT US!- WHAT'LL WE DO?- BETTER GET YOUR PROVERBS WORKIN'!
WELL OILED MACHINERY GUN MUCH HANDIER THAN PLOVERB AT PLESENT! - HOWSOEVER..
MILTON CANIFF
...MAN WHO RIDES TIGER MUST BE CAREFUL NOT TO LET GO!- MEBBE WISE TO PLAY SLEEPY LIKE PUSSY CAT!- THEN. WHEN RAT IS FULL OF CHEESE, WE JUMP- AN' RAT IS JUS' WASBEEN!
Reg. U. S. Pat. Off.: Copyright, 1936, by Chicago Tribune-N. Y. News Syndicate, Inc.

WITH PAT SENT UNCONSCIOUS TO THE BOILER ROOM, TERRY AND CONNIE ARE LEFT ALONE TO TRY TO PUZZLE OUT A MEANS OF ESCAPE FROM THE OIL TANKER–THEY DECIDE TO PLAY A WAITING GAME.....
1-13
REMEMBER, CONNIE, WE TAKE ORDERS AN' WAIT FOR A BREAK!
SHH! COMES EVIL SAILOR!
YOU GO ON DECK, SUDDEN!
YOU TAKE BRUSH! SCRUB DECK 'TIL SHINE GOOD!
WHAT? -WHY THIS OIL'S AN INCH THICK!
Reg. U. S. Pat. Off.; Copyright, 1936, by Chicago Tribune-N. Y. News Syndicate, Inc.
SO YOU SCRUB OFF INCH OF OIL AN' MAKE SHINE! DO SUDDEN!
MOST PEOPLE POUR OIL ON TH' WATERS WHEN THEY'RE IN TROUBLE! – NOT US! –WE GET IN TROUBLE AN' CRAWL IN TH' OIL!
MILTON CANIFF

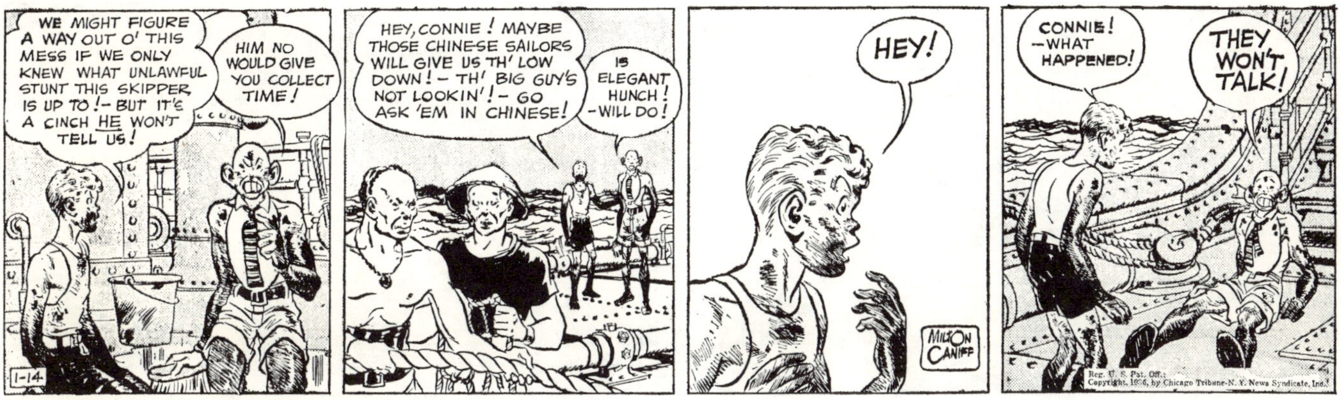
WE MIGHT FIGURE A WAY OUT O' THIS MESS IF WE ONLY KNEW WHAT UNLAWFUL STUNT THIS SKIPPER IS UP TO! – BUT IT'S A CINCH HE WON'T TELL US!
HIM NO WOULD GIVE YOU COLLECT TIME!
1-14
HEY, CONNIE! MAYBE THOSE CHINESE SAILORS WILL GIVE US TH' LOW DOWN! – TH' BIG GUY'S NOT LOOKIN'! – GO ASK 'EM IN CHINESE!
IS ELEGANT HUNCH! -WILL DO!
HEY!
MILTON CANIFF
CONNIE! -WHAT HAPPENED!
THEY WON'T TALK!
Reg. U. S. Pat. Off.; Copyright, 1936, by Chicago Tribune-N. Y. News Syndicate, Inc.

FOR DAYS TERRY AND CONNIE ARE WORKED LIKE DOGS ON THE OIL TANKER ... BUT THEY DO NOT PROTEST, HOPING THEIR CHANCE WILL COME ....
THEY WON'T LET US SEE PAT OR ANYTHING! GEE, IT'S DRIVIN' ME LOONEY!
EVIL ONE SAY MIST' PAT OKAY AN' WORKIN' IN BOILER ROOM!
1-15
YEAH – BUT IF WE COULD JUS' TALK TO HIM! – THEN WE COULD FIGURE OUT A WAY TO ESCAPE!
WHO TRAVELS FASTEST FALLS HARDEST! – WE WAIT! – SOON MEBBE GET IDEA WHAT'S IT ALL ABOUT!
MILTON CANIFF
HEY LITTLE ONE! – MASTER SAY YOU COME SERVE HIS DINNER LIKE CABIN BOY!
WHO'S A LITTLE ONE, YAH BIG OX?
Reg. U. S. Pat. Off.; Copyright, 1936, by Chicago Tribune-N. Y. News Syndicate, Inc.
SHH! – YOU DO LIKE HE SAY! – GOTTA GET NEAR MACHINERY TO FLING MONKEY WRENCHES IN SAME!
YOU'RE RIGHT, CONFUCIUS! I'M OFF TO BEARD TH' LION! – ONLY THIS ONE'S GOT A GOATEE!

I'VE BROUGHT YOUR DINNER LIKE YOU SAID!
AH, THE FIERY YOUNG WILDCAT HAS BECOME A GENTLE LAMB!
1-16
I SUPPOSE YOU WERE CAREFUL TO POISON MY FOOD BEFORE YOU BROUGHT IT HERE! – ISN'T THAT THE USUAL PROCEDURE?
WOULD BE – BUT I USED UP ALL MY POISON ON TH' LAST VILLAIN I MET!
IF THIS WERE THE CINEMA I SHOULD HAVE YOU TORTURED FOR YOUR IMPUDENCE! – BUT YOU AMUSE ME! – NOW LEAVE ME TO MY APPETITE!
OKAY!
MILTON CANIFF
Reg. U. S. Pat. Off.; Copyright, 1936, by Chicago Tribune-N. Y. News Syndicate, Inc.
AS TERRY TURNS TO GO, SOMETHING CATCHES HIS EYE THAT MAKES HIM STIFLE A CRY — THEN LEAVE IN A BIG HURRY....

1-17
CONNIE! I SAW IT! I SAW IT!
WHAT SEE? SPOOK MEBBE? -WHISPER QUIET! WALLS HAVE EAR TRUMPETS!
NOT THAT! - IT WAS A MONTH OLD ENGLISH NEWSPAPER FROM SHANGHAI! -'ON TH' DESK IN TH' SKIPPER'S CABIN!
MEBBE CONNIE DON'T THINK SO GOOD! -NO CATCH IDEA
MILTON CANIFF
Reg. U. S. Pat. Off.
Copyright, 1936, by Chicago Tribune-N. Y. News Syndicate, Inc.
I JUST HAD A QUICK GLANCE - BUT TH' HEADLINE SAID 'PIRATES LOOT STEAMER IN NEW OUTBREAK! - RAIDERS HEAD FOR OPEN SEA IN NATIVE JUNKS AFTER FIRING VESSEL' !!
OL' DUMB CONNIE! - STILL DON'T QUITE SEE WHY SUCH IMPORTANCE!
IT'S THAT LINE - 'RAIDERS HEAD FOR OPEN SEA IN NATIVE JUNKS' - I'VE GOT IT, PAL, I'VE GOT IT!

1-18
YOU READ 'BOUT PIRATES GOIN' TO OPEN SEA AFTER BIG HOLDUP! - CONNIE DON'T SEE TIEUP WITH PLESANT WOEFUL DILEMA!
LISTEN! - PIRATES DON'T HEAD FOR OPEN WATER AFTER A BIG HAUL...
...THEY SCOOT FOR SOME SHALLOW RIVER WHERE TH' GUNBOATS CAN'T FOLLOW 'EM! - THEN THEY TRY TO HIDE THEIR BOOTY! - BUT IT'S USUALLY FOUND AN' TH' PIRATES SHOT!...
IS TRUE! PIRACY VELLY UNHEALTHY BUSINESS!
WHAT'S TO PREVENT SOME SMART GUY RUNNING WHAT APPEARS T' BE A LEGITIMATE VESSEL ALONG TH' COAST WHERE THOSE PIRATES CAN DUMP THEIR SWAG AN' NOT WORRY 'BOUT IT BEIN' FOUND!
YOU MEAN...
Reg. U. S. Pat. Off.
Copyright, 1936, by Chicago Tribune-N. Y. News Syndicate, Inc.
I MEAN A FLOATING TREASURE ISLAND! THAT'S WHY THOSE JUNKS WENT TO SEA - TO LEAVE THEIR GOLD ON SUCH A SHIP! - AND THIS IS IT!
MILTON CANIFF

TAKING A CLUE FROM AN OLD NEWSPAPER IN THE CAPTAIN'S CABIN, TERRY REASONS THAT HE AND PAT AND CONNIE ARE PRISONERS ON THE MOTHER SHIP FOR A FLEET OF SMALL PIRATE BOATS WHICH HAVE BEEN TERRORIZING THE CHINA COAST....
1-20
YOU MEAN EVIL PIRATE FELLERS ROB SHIPS - AN' BLING LOOT TO THIS SMELLY OL' OIL TANKER?
SURE, IT'S A PERFECT COVER-UP! - A FLOATING TREASURE ISLAND!
JIMMINY WHIZ! IF SUCH IS SO - AN' TANKER IS CAPTURED - WE GET BOOM SHOT LIKE PIRATE GENTS! VELLY UNHOTSY DANDY!
RIGHT! - WE GOTTA GET PAT OUTA THAT ENGINE ROOM AN' ESCAPE FROM THIS SCOW SOME WAY!
Reg. U. S. Pat. Off.
Copyright, 1936, by Chicago Tribune-N. Y. News Syndicate, Inc.
LOOK! - IS CHIEF ENGINE FELLER GOIN' TO SKIPPER'S CABIN! MONKEYSHINES ON FOOT, I BETCHA!
TRY AN DUCK AROUND BY TH WINDOW! - HERE'S WHERE WE GET TH' LOW DOWN!
MILTON CANIFF

AS THE CHIEF ENGINEER ENTERS THE CAPTAIN'S CABIN, TERRY AND CONNIE CROUCH UNDER THE OPEN WINDOW....
1-21
AH - A VISIT FROM MY HIGHLY EFFICIENT CHIEF ENGINEER! - WHAT PROBLEM VEXES YOUR NOBLE BRAIN TONIGHT, GOOD SIR?
LISTEN, JUDAS! - I WANTS T' KNOW WHEN WE'RE PUTTIN' INTO PORT T' DIVIDE TH' SWAG WE GOT ABOARD? - I'M TIRED WAITIN' FER MY DOUGH!
DON'T USE THAT TONE WITH ME! - I'M MISTER JUDAS TO YOU! - AND I'M GIVING THE ORDERS HERE!
Reg. U. S. Pat. Off.
Copyright, 1936, by Chicago Tribune-N. Y. News Syndicate, Inc.
MILTON CANIFF
FER PETE'S SAKE! - HIS NAME IS JUDAS! HOLD YOUR BREATH - ANYTHING'S LIABLE T' HAPPEN!

ALL RIGHT MISTER JUDAS!—WE GOT A FORTUNE ABOARD THAT THEM CHINEE PIRATES HAVE TOOK FROM VARIOUS SHIPS!—WHEN DO I GIT MY CUT?
SO—THE SMELL OF GOLD BRINGS OUT THE GREED!
1-22
T' BLAZES WITH THEM HIGH SOUNDIN' WORDS! —YOU KNOW TH' BRITISH AN' FRENCH SHIPS IS BOUND T'CATCH ON T' US SOON!—I'M FER SPLITTIN' UP AN HEADIN' FER AMERICA!
TUT! TUT! YOU'RE JUST NERVOUS!
HOWEVER!—TONIGHT AT TWELVE OUR MEN RAID THE STEAMER JUNG FU OFF BLUE BIRD ISLAND—THEY WILL BRING THEIR HAUL ON BOARD HERE AS USUAL!—THEN WE WILL MAKE FOR OUR BASE AND YOU WILL RECEIVE YOUR SHARE!
ALL RIGHT!—SEE THAT YOU DON'T TRY T' SQUEEZE ME OUT, MISTER JUDAS!
OOOH! TONIGHT IS FIREWORKS AN' WE SITTIN' ON BIGGEST CANNON CLACKER!
MILTON CANIFF
Reg. U. S. Pat. Off.; Copyright, 1936, by Chicago Tribune-N. Y. News Syndicate, Inc.

I TRUST YOUR ALL CONSUMING GREED WILL BE SATISFIED BY TONIGHT'S HAUL!
CALL IT ANY FANCY NAMES Y' LIKE—AFTER T'NIGHT I WANT A PAY-OFF!
1-23
YOU ATTEND YOUR ENGINES AND LEAVE THE THINKING TO ME!—GO BELOW!
OKAY!
GOTCHA!
WHAT'S THAT?
HEY! GLUB!
OOOCH!
I KETCHUM MAKE LISTEN BY WINDOW—SHOULD CHOP OFF HEADS—OR TOSSUM TO SHARKS—OR BOTH?
MILTON CANIFF

THEY LISTEN BY WINDOW WHILE MASTER TALK TO ENGINE CHIEF! —I KILLUM—HUH?
OUCH! LEGGO MY NECK!
1-24
INDEED!—SO WE HAVE A MODERN JIM HAWKINS WHO LISTENS FROM THE APPLE BARREL TO TALK OF PIRACY—JUST AS IN "TREASURE ISLAND"!
Reg. U. S. Pat. Off.; Copyright, 1936, by Chicago Tribune-N. Y. News Syndicate, Inc.
ROBERT LOUIS STEVENSON COULD HARDLY HAVE GUESSED THAT HIS YOUNG HERO WOULD HAVE A 1936 COUNTERPART! —THIS IS WHIMSICAL, NO END!
MILTON CANIFF
WHIMSICAL, MY EYE!—YOU'RE A BIGGER PIRATE THAN LONG JOHN SILVER EVER DREAMED OF BEIN'! —AN' IF YOU'RE CAPTURED WE'LL BE SHOT RIGHT ALONG WITH YOU!
YOUR COMPARISON FLATTERS ME!—AS FOR US ALL BEING SHOT—YOU'RE QUITE RIGHT!

WELL—YOU CAUGHT US LISTENIN' AT YOUR WINDOW—AN' WE KNOW YOU'RE TH' BRAINS OF A PIRATE MOB—NOW WHAT?
GETTING ANXIOUS, EH?
1-25
YOU TWO, AND YOUR FRIEND IN THE ENGINE ROOM ARE HUSKY LADS—I CAN USE YOU AS LABORERS—BUT YOU'D BE LESS DANGEROUS WITH YOUR TONGUES CUT OUT!
WHAT?
OH WOE!
CAPTAIN JUDAS! COME QUICK!
Reg. U. S. Pat. Off.; Copyright, 1936, by Chicago Tribune-N. Y. News Syndicate, Inc.
GLOW IN SKY!—MEANS STEAMER HAS BEEN RAIDED!—MEN WILL COME SOON WITH LOOT!
ORDER ALL HANDS ON DECK!
MILTON CANIFF

CAUGHT LISTENING UNDER CAPTAIN JUDAS' WINDOW, TERRY AND CONNIE ARE IN A DESPERATE SPOT—WHEN A SAILOR BURSTS IN ANNOUNCING THE COMING OF THE PIRATE FLEET TO UNLOAD ITS BOOTY ON THE OIL TANKER!
1-27
CAPTAIN JUDAS RUSHES TO THE BRIDGE, LEAVING TERRY AND CONNIE ALONE....
OOOH! LUCK! HE JUST ABOUT TO WHACK OUT TONGUES—THEN HE GO SUDDEN!
NOW'S OUR CHANCE TO BEAT IT! STEP ON IT, CONNIE!
Reg. U. S. Pat. Off.: Copyright, 1936, by Chicago Tribune-N. Y. News Syndicate, Inc.
TH' WHOLE CREW'S WATCHIN' FOR TH' PIRATE JUNKS T' COME ALONGSIDE. THEY WON'T NOTICE US!
BUT, MIST' PAT—HE IN OL' BOILEE ROOM DOWN DEEP!
MILTON CANIFF
I KNOW!—IT'S A LONG GAMBLE, BUT WE MIGHT MAKE IT!—FOLLOW ME, AN' DO AS I SAY!
YOU SAYUM—I DOUM! CONNIE COME CLIPPITY BANGITY!

ON THE BRIDGE OF THE PIRATE OIL TANKER....
ARE WE IN THE EXACT POSITION AGREED UPON?
YES, MASTER—EVEN NOW COMES JUNKS IN NIGHT!
1-28
THE ONLY GUY WE GOTTA FEAR BELOW IS TH' CHIEF ENGINEER—IF WE CUT OFF TH' ENGINE ROOM FROM THE BRIDGE WE CAN CRIPPLE THE SHIP!
HE VELLY BIGGISH GENT!—HOW WE DO HIM UNDER?
Reg. U. S. Pat. Off.: Copyright, 1936, by Chicago Tribune-N. Y. News Syndicate, Inc.
THERE'LL BE A HOSE ON THE BOILER WITH LIVE STEAM IN IT! IF WE CAN GET HOLD OF THAT!
I GITCHA! I GITCHA!—HERE DOOR! SHUSH QUIET!
MILTON CANIFF
IN THE ENGINE ROOM THE CHIEF DRIVES PAT AND THE COOLIES TO GET UP STEAM FOR A HURRIED ESCAPE AFTER THE BOOTY IS TAKEN ABOARD!

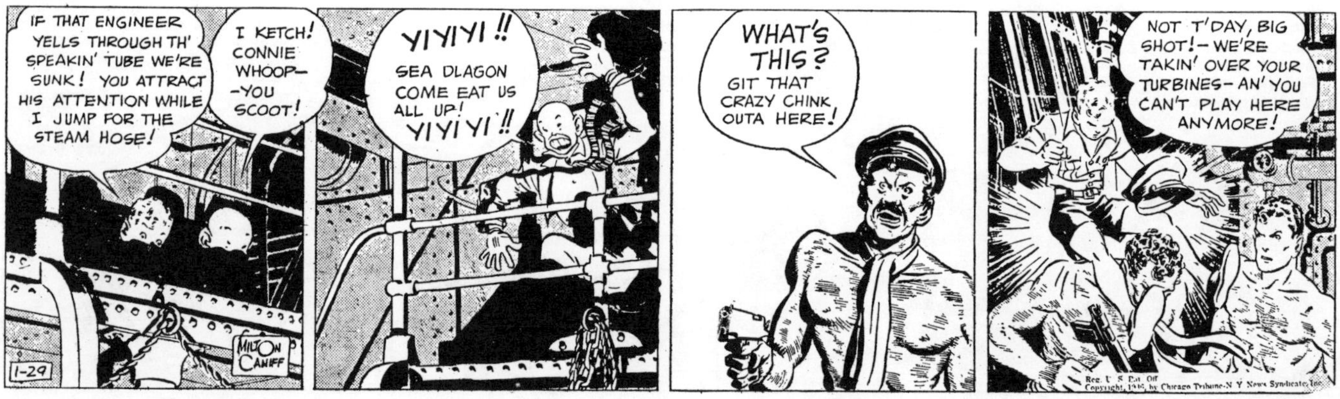
IF THAT ENGINEER YELLS THROUGH TH' SPEAKIN' TUBE WE'RE SUNK! YOU ATTRACT HIS ATTENTION WHILE I JUMP FOR THE STEAM HOSE!
I KETCH! CONNIE WHOOP—YOU SCOOT!
MILTON CANIFF
1-29
YIYIYI!! SEA DLAGON COME EAT US ALL UP! YIYIYI!!
WHAT'S THIS? GIT THAT CRAZY CHINK OUTA HERE!
NOT T'DAY, BIG SHOT!—WE'RE TAKIN' OVER YOUR TURBINES—AN' YOU CAN'T PLAY HERE ANYMORE!
Reg. U. S. Pat. Off. Copyright, 1936, by Chicago Tribune-N. Y. News Syndicate, Inc.

TERRY! WHAT'S HAPPENED?
IT'S OUR CHANCE TO ESCAPE—WRECK THAT SPEAKIN' TUBE BEFORE THIS GUY COMES TO!
1-30
THIS TANKER'S A FLOATING TREASURE ISLAND—PIRATE JUNKS ALONGSIDE NOW TO UNLOAD GOLD! IF WE WRECK THESE ENGINES AND GRAB A JUNK THEY CAN'T FOLLOW US—
YOU SMASH THE ENGINES—I'LL HOLD THOSE NATIVES BACK WITH TH' STEAM HOSE!
MOST OF THE NATIVE STOKERS ARE DAZED BY THE SUDDEN TURN OF EVENTS—BUT ONE HAS CREPT AROUND BEHIND TERRY AND PAT...
MILTON CANIFF
Reg. U. S. Pat. Off. Copyright, 1936, by Chicago Tribune-N. Y. News Syndicate, Inc.

As Pat wrecks the tanker's engines and Terry holds the stokers at bay— one of the natives crawls around behind them...
1-31
PAT! PAT! LOOK OUT!
Is ol' dizzly Connie's Sunday pitch! —— Call um Chinese bean ball! —You like pletty good?
Reg. U. S. Pat. Off.: Copyright, 1936, by Chicago Tribune-N. Y. News Syndicate, Inc.
Milton Caniff

The tanker's engines and speaking tube wrecked, Terry, Pat and Connie barricade the boiler room door and go on deck...
Th' junks are already alongside with their loot!
2-1
Captain Judas and his crew are too busy loading the stuff to notice the engine room's cut off!
We couldn't get away with a life boat!— One of those junks is our only out!
Milton Caniff
Slip over the side and swim to a junk on the fringe of the fleet! —We may get shot— but it's worth trying!
Don't make a sound— if anyone's hit the others run for it! — There's a good wind! — Get in that junk and head for shore, 'cause the devil's on your heels!

While Captain Judas and his crew are busy unloading booty from the pirate junks, Terry, Pat and Connie slip over the side and swim to a native craft on the fringe of the cluster around the tanker...
2-3
Just one guard on this baby! I'll get 'im! -You cast off!
Reg. U. S. Pat. Off.: Copyright, 1936, by Chicago Tribune-N. Y. News Syndicate, Inc.
Milton Caniff
The lone junk slips away from the pack — but a sailor sees it, and the cat is out of the bag!....
Master! Master! I seeum! White men steal boat!

Master! Look sudden!-White men steal junk-go to shore!
2-4
It's those accursed prisoners! I should have shot them! Give me full steam ahead!
Master! No answer from below -Levers don't work!
Reg. U. S. Pat. Off.: Copyright, 1936, by Chicago Tribune-N. Y. News Syndicate, Inc.
At this moment the chief engineer stumbles to the bridge...
Judas! They've jimmied me engines! We're helpless!
After them, in the junks! -If they reach shore we ALL die! —Shoot them down, you fools! -Or your heads will hang in the public square!
Milton Caniff

THEY'RE AFTER US, BUT THEY'LL HAVE NO MORE WIND THAN WE! — GIVE 'ER EVERY INCH OF SAIL!
2-5
SCUDDING ALONG BEFORE A STIFF BREEZE, THREE JUNKS ARE ON THE TRAIL OF THE FLEEING PRISONERS...
Reg. U. S. Pat. Off.: Copyright, 1936, by Chicago Tribune-N. Y. News Syndicate, Inc.
OOOH! BOOM GUNS POP PLENTY! — SCOOT LIKE HUM BIRD, LI'L JUNKY! CONNIE WANTA GET FROM HENCE VELLY SUDDEN!
MILTON CANIFF
I'VE GOT SIX SHOTS IN THIS GUN — WE'LL SAVE EM! — IF THESE GUYS CATCH US THEY'LL BE SCREAMIN' FOR OUR BLOOD! — BUT SIX OF 'EM WILL SEE THEIR OWN FIRST!!

THE PIRATE JUNKS, NAVIGATED BY EXPERTS, SLOWLY CLOSE IN ON TERRY, PAT AND CONNIE....
THEY'RE COMIN' CLOSER — AND I CAN'T GET A BIT MORE SPEED OUT O' THIS SCOW!
2-6
NOT ONLY THAT BUT IT'S GETTIN' DAYLIGHT! — WHEN THEY GET WITHIN RANGE THEY'LL OPEN FIRE AGAIN!
WOULD GIVE MUCH THANKS FOR NICE BIG SUBMALINE AT PLESENT MOMENT!
AS THE PIRATES BEAR DOWN ON THEIR PREY, THEY MAN THE RAILS, CROUCHED FOR THE KILL....
MILTON CANIFF
Reg. U. S. Pat. Off.: Copyright, 1936, by Chicago Tribune-N. Y. News Syndicate, Inc.

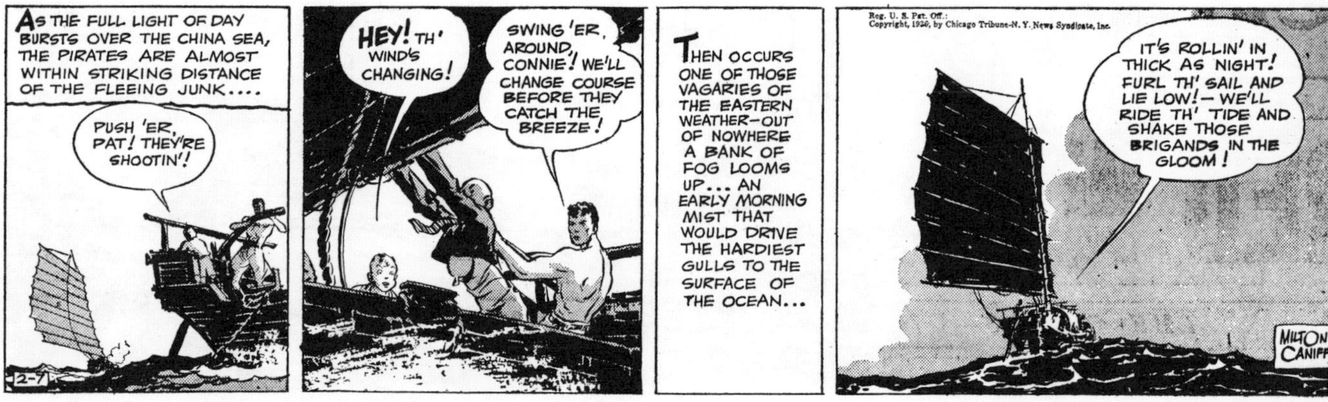
AS THE FULL LIGHT OF DAY BURSTS OVER THE CHINA SEA, THE PIRATES ARE ALMOST WITHIN STRIKING DISTANCE OF THE FLEEING JUNK....
PUSH 'ER, PAT! THEY'RE SHOOTIN'!
2-7
HEY! TH' WIND'S CHANGING!
SWING 'ER AROUND, CONNIE! WE'LL CHANGE COURSE BEFORE THEY CATCH THE BREEZE!
THEN OCCURS ONE OF THOSE VAGARIES OF THE EASTERN WEATHER — OUT OF NOWHERE A BANK OF FOG LOOMS UP... AN EARLY MORNING MIST THAT WOULD DRIVE THE HARDIEST GULLS TO THE SURFACE OF THE OCEAN...
Reg. U. S. Pat. Off.: Copyright, 1936, by Chicago Tribune-N. Y. News Syndicate, Inc.
IT'S ROLLIN' IN THICK AS NIGHT! FURL TH' SAIL AND LIE LOW! — WE'LL RIDE TH' TIDE AND SHAKE THOSE BRIGANDS IN THE GLOOM!
MILTON CANIFF

HOORAY! THE FOG'S FOLDIN' US UP LIKE A BABE IN ARMS! — WE'LL LOSE TH' PIRATES NOW!
2-8
QUIET, TERRY! THEY'LL SHOOT IN THE DIRECTION OF THE SOUND!
LISTEN! THEY SHOOTIN' NOW! — BUT NOT AT US! IS GOOD! — IS HOTSY DANDY!
Reg. U. S. Pat. Off.: Copyright, 1936, by Chicago Tribune-N. Y. News Syndicate, Inc.
THEY EXPECTED US TO BACKTRACK! — WE'LL CROSS 'EM BY GOING STRAIGHT AHEAD! —
YEAH — BUT JUST WHERE ARE WE GOIN'? — WHICH DIRECTION IS SHORE — AN' WHICH IS OPEN SEA?
MILTON CANIFF
WHEN THE FOG LIFTS WE CAN SAIL BY THE SUN — BUT WHERE WE'LL LAND, I DON'T KNOW — YOUR GUESS IS AS GOOD AS MINE!
OOH JOY! — MAY SAIL TO UNITED STATES — LAND IN HOLLYWOODS! — SEE BOOTIFUL ACTRESS LADIES! — 4000 MILES! HMMM! — GET MIGHTY HUNGLY IN MEANTIME!

THANKFUL FOR THE FOG THAT HAS HIDDEN THEM FROM THEIR PURSUERS, TERRY, PAT AND CONNIE PUSH ON BEFORE THE STEADY WIND...
HAVING NO COMPASS, THEY DON'T KNOW WHETHER THEY MOVE TOWARD SHORE - OR THE OPEN SEA...
2-10
SPEAK IN WHISPERS! - TH' PIRATE JUNKS MAY BE ONLY A FEW YARDS AWAY!
IF TH' SUN COMES OUT IT'LL LIFT THIS MURK - AN' WE'LL BE OUT O' LUCK!
WE'RE RUNNING AHEAD OF THE SAME WIND THAT'S MOVING THE FOG BANK - WE'LL STAY IN IT IF IT DOESN'T MELT!
FUNNY DOIN'S! - MOST SEA CHAPS SCARED O' FOGS! - WE HUGGUM LIKE LONG LOST PAL CHUM!
SAY - I'M GETTIN' HUNGRY AN' THIRSTY! - WE CAN'T GO ON LIKE THIS FOR LONG! - WE'LL BE CHEWIN' UP TH' SAILS!
IS SO! RIBS PLAY TUNE ON BACKBONE!
SSHH! I HEARD A SPLASH! - DON'T SAY A WORD! LIE FLAT!
MILTON CANIFF
Reg. U. S. Pat. Off.: Copyright, 1936, by Chicago Tribune-N. Y. News Syndicate, Inc.

WHATSA MATTER, PAT?
- HEARD A SPLASH! MIGHT BE AN OAR! - KEEP QUIET!
2-11
ALMOST AFRAID TO BREATHE, TERRY, PAT AND CONNIE LIE IN THEIR BOAT AS THE FOG SWIRLS SILENTLY ABOUT THEM..
MILTON CANIFF
HOLD OARS!
WHAT IS? - YOU SEE MELICANS MAYBE?
DON'T KNOW! - THINK PLERHAPS HEAR VOICE! - ROW THAT WAY!
Reg. U. S. Pat. Off.: Copyright, 1936, by Chicago Tribune-N. Y. News Syndicate, Inc.

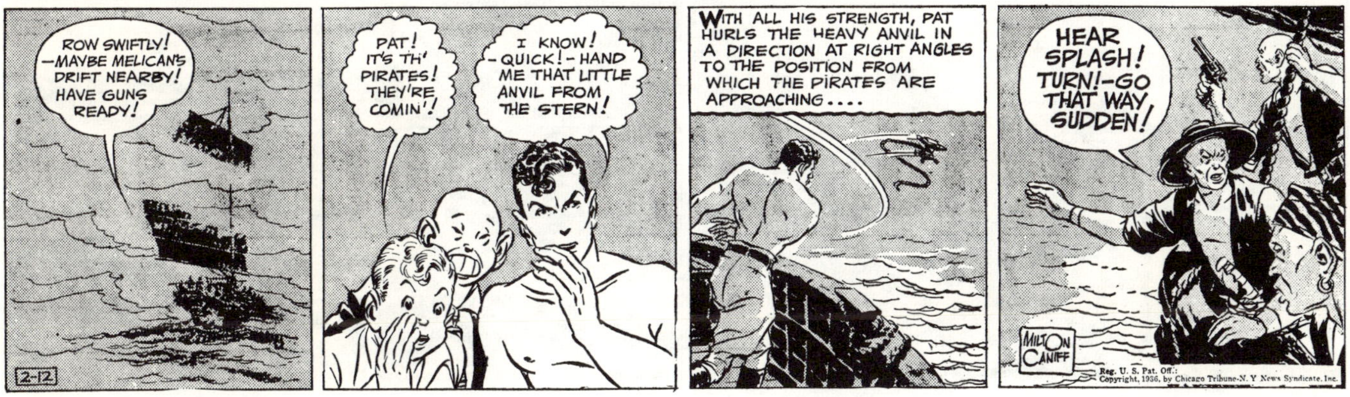
ROW SWIFTLY! - MAYBE MELICANS DRIFT NEARBY! HAVE GUNS READY!
2-12
PAT! IT'S TH' PIRATES! THEY'RE COMIN'!
I KNOW! - QUICK! - HAND ME THAT LITTLE ANVIL FROM THE STERN!
WITH ALL HIS STRENGTH, PAT HURLS THE HEAVY ANVIL IN A DIRECTION AT RIGHT ANGLES TO THE POSITION FROM WHICH THE PIRATES ARE APPROACHING....
MILTON CANIFF
HEAR SPLASH! TURN! - GO THAT WAY SUDDEN!
Reg. U. S. Pat. Off.: Copyright, 1936, by Chicago Tribune-N. Y. News Syndicate, Inc.

PAT THROWS AN ANVIL FAR OUT IN THE SEA TO MISLEAD THE APPROACHING PIRATE CRAFT!
BIG SPLASH! SHOOTUM!
2-13
THEY FELL FOR IT! THEY'RE SHOOTIN' TOWARD TH' SPLASH!
ROW, YOU GUYS - WHILE THEY'RE WHOOPIN' IT UP! - WE GOTTA GET AWAY FROM HERE!
FOR HOURS THEY BEND OVER THE OARS, PUTTING OPEN WATER BETWEEN THEM AND THEIR PURSUERS
GOLLY PAT, I GOTTA STOP! - I'M GETTIN' DIZZY!
MILTON CANIFF
CONNIE TOO! - OH FOR BIG DLINK O' COLD WATER!
I THINK WE'VE SHAKEN THOSE CUT-THROATS! - NOW WE'VE GOT TO GET TO SHORE BEFORE WE GO BATTY AND DRINK SALT WATER!
Reg. U. S. Pat. Off.: Copyright, 1936, by Chicago Tribune-N. Y. News Syndicate, Inc.

2-14
AFTER THEIR LONG PULL, TERRY, PAT AND CONNIE FALL INTO AN EXHAUSTED SLUMBER—WHEN THEY AWAKEN THE FOG HAS LIFTED AND IT IS PITCH DARK...
OH BOY! DID I SLEEP! HEY YOU GUYS! WAKE UP!
I WAS AFRAID OF THIS!—WE'VE SLEPT THROUGH THE DAY, AND NOW WITH AN OVERCAST SKY WE CAN'T SAIL BY THE STARS!
MIST' CHRISTO COLUMBO SAW LI'L BERRIES FLOATIN' WHEN HE GOT CLOSE TO LAND!
LISTEN TO BRIGHT EYES! —HE'S BEEN READIN' BOOKS AGAIN!
MAYBE A BREADFRUIT TREE WILL FLOAT BY!—THEN WE CAN FIND OUR WAY AND HAVE BREAKFAST TOO!
MILTON CANIFF
AW-YOU MAKE FUN! —CONNIE ONLY TLY TO HELP UNHAPPY FLIX!
SORRY, PAL!—GUESS WE'RE GETTIN' SORT O' DAFFY FROM THIS SUSPENSE! WE CAN USE ANY SUGGESTION TO TRY AND REACH SHORE.. —HEY!—THE WIND'S PICKING UP!—
Reg. U. S. Pat. Off.: Copyright, 1936, by Chicago Tribune-N. Y. News Syndicate, Inc.

2-15
WOW! TH' WIND'S HOWLIN' LIKE A TYPHOON! —LISTEN TO THAT MAST CREAK!
WE'LL RIDE ALONG WITH THE BREEZE! —MAY DRIVE US IN TO SHORE!
OOOOH! MEBBE OL' SWORD FISH COME UP AN' CUT HOLE IN BASEMENT OF BOAT!— THEN, POOF!—ALL SINK TO MIST' DAVID JONES LOCKER ROOM!
LISTEN! —HEAR THAT RUMBLE? IT'S GETTIN' LOUDER!
SURF! —MEANS ROCKS AHEAD!—WE'RE GOIN' STRAIGHT FOR EM!—STAND BY TO BAIL!
MILTON CANIFF
WHITE WATER AHEAD!—WE'RE SCRAPIN' BOTTOM! WOW! FURL THAT SAIL!
FORGET TH' SAIL! EVERY MAN FOR HIMSELF! WE'RE GOIN' OVER!
Reg. U. S. Pat. Off. Copyright, 1936, by Chicago Tribune N Y News Syndicate, Inc.

STEERING BLINDLY IN THE DARK, TERRY, PAT AND CONNIE ARE THROWN INTO THE SURF AS THEIR CAPTURED JUNK CRASHES AGAINST THE ROCKY SHORE... FRANTICALLY THEY BATTLE THE UNDERTOW THAT THREATENS TO PULL THEM BACK TO DEEP WATER...
2-17
GLUB! I SWALLOWED MOST O' TH' PACIFIC!
SWIM FOR IT!—GRAB A ROCK, AN' HANG ON!
OW! MY HEAD! —HELP!
GOTCHA PAL!
WITH A DESPERATE BURST OF STRENGTH, PAT PULLS TERRY TO THE SHORE AND THEY BOTH LIE EXHAUSTED FROM THE ORDEAL...
MILTON CANIFF

WOW!—I FEEL LIKE A FOOTBALL AFTER A HARD GAME! TERRY!—YOU ALL RIGHT?
HUNH? —OH—YEAH —I MUST HAVE BEEN KNOCKED DIZZY!
2-18
Reg. U. S. Pat. Off.: Copyright, 1936, by Chicago Tribune-N. Y. News Syndicate, Inc.
YOU WERE—! —AND I'M SO WEAK FROM HUNGER I MUST HAVE PASSED OUT TOO!
I SOAKED UP SO MUCH BRINE I FEEL LIKE A DILL PICKLE! —HEY!—WHERE'S CONNIE?
I DUNNO! —GEE—DO YOU SUPPOSE..? —HEY! WHAT'S THAT!
YOOWHOZE! —GIVE LOOK— —IS MOST EMBARRASSFUL, PLEDICKLYMENT!
MILTON CANIFF
HOW DO! HOW DO! —IS ME!—ALL SUDDEN HOOK CATCHUM IN BRITCHES AN' UP GOES CONNIE!— —GOTTA DLY OUT SOMEHOW ANYHOW, SAYS ME... SO HERE BE ME—AT HALF MAST!

GUESS WE'RE ALL THREE LUCKY TO GET ASHORE ALIVE! – THE JUNK'S A WRECK! –GOOD FOR NOTHING BUT FIREWOOD!
IF WE COULD SHOOT SOME GAME WE COULD EAT A WELL COOKED MEAL, ANYHOW!
2-19
I'M GLAD I GRABBED THIS GUN! – I'LL TRY TO GET SOME OF THE WATER OUT OF IT!
–WONDER IF THIS IS AN ISLAND OR THE MAINLAND?
Reg. U. S. Pat. Off. Copyright, 1936, by Chicago Tribune-N. Y. News Syndicate, Inc.
MILTON CANIFF
LOOK LIKE ISLAND WHERE WEAZEL CAPTURED MISSY NORMANDIE DLAKE! –REMEMBER..? OW!
WHAT DID YOU SAY, CONNIE?
AH– HE SAID HE'D SURE BE ENRAPTURED BY AN ENORMOUS STEAK! – DIDN'T YOU CONNIE?
–OH SHOO! SHOO MIKE!

FROM THE WAY THIS SHORE CURVES WE MUST BE ON AN ISLAND–BUT WE'RE TOO WEAK TO CARRY ON!
YOU SAID IT, PAL!
2-20
AN' WE HAVEN'T EVEN SEEN A LONESOME GOPHER TO SHOOT AT! –BOY THIS IS REALLY A BARREN ISLAND!
I'D EVEN LIKE TO SEE A TRIBE OF CANNIBALS! –AT LEAST THEY'D FATTEN US UP BEFORE THEY ATE US!
MANY CHINESE MUST SCRATCH LIVING FROM WOEFUL LAND LIKE THUS! – NO WONDER THEY BECOME EVIL BANDIT FELLERS! –CHINESE UNHAPPY PEOPLE!
MILTON CANIFF
GUESS YOU'RE RIGHT, CONNIE! – WE'LL CAMP HERE FOR THE NIGHT! – BETTER SLEEP FAR APART! – SOMEBODY MIGHT DREAM OF A BIG STEAK AND TAKE A BITE OUT OF THE NEAREST LEG! –REST HEAPTY LADS, YOU'LL NEED YOUR STRENGTH!

HUNGRY, THIRSTY AND TIRED, THE BOYS FALL ASLEEP ON THE BEACH –HOURS PASS–THEN TERRY WAKES WITH A START...
WHUZZAT?
MILTON CANIFF
2-21
PAT! WAKE UP!
HUH?– WHAT'S EATIN' YOU, TERRY?
LISTEN, PAL! DO YOU HEAR IT?
–HEAR WHAT?– ARE YA GOIN' CRAZY!
NO! NO! –BE QUIET –LISTEN A MINUTE! –DO YOU HEAR IT?
....WHY– WHY–SURE I HEAR IT! – IT'S MUSIC! – SOMEBODY'S PLAYIN' A RECORD OF TH' ST. LOUIS BLUES!

A LONELY ISLAND ON TH' CHINA COAST –AN' SOMEBODY'S PLAYIN' A RECORD OF TH' ST. LOUIS BLUES!!
OR IT MIGHT BE A RADIO! –ANYWAY IT'S PEOPLE COME ON!
2-22
HUH! WHERE GO? HOW COMES? –IS DLEAM?
NO DREAM!– WE'VE GOT NEIGHBORS! –AN' IF THEY'VE GOT A PHONOGRAPH, THEY'VE GOT A CAN O' BEANS! – SHAKE A LEG!
YIPPEE! – A HOUSE AND A LIGHT! – RUN, YOU BEACHCOMBERS! –LAST MAN THERE GETS THE LEAVINGS!
I'LL KNOCK ON THE DOOR!
WAIT, PAT! LOOK! – IN TH' WINDOW!
WELL FER MERCY GOO'NESS, AN' NO FOOLIN'S!
MILTON CANIFF

TERRY, PAT AND CONNIE ARE AWAKENED BY THE DISTANT SOUND OF A PHONOGRAPH OR RADIO, PLAYING "ST. LOUIS BLUES"
RUNNING UP FROM THE BEACH, THEY SEE A HOUSE... APPROACHING THE LIGHTED WINDOW, THEY STOP SHORT...
2-24
LET'S ASK FOR SOME FOOD! - I'M STARVED!
WELL! WELL! WELL! WELL! WELL!
WAIT, PAT! - LOOK IN TH' WINDOW!
Reg. U. S. Pat. Off.: Copyright, 1936, by Chicago Tribune-N. Y. News Syndicate, Inc.
WHAT'S TH' HOLDUP? HEY! - IS THAT REAL - OR AM I DREAMIN'?
AN' WE THOUGHT THIS WAS A DESERTED ISLAND! - HMMM!
... AND IT'S LITTLE WONDER THE BOYS ARE SURPRISED - FOR INSIDE THE LONELY HOUSE THEY SEE....
MILTON CANIFF

LUVVA PETE! - A PRETTY BLONDE, DANCIN' ALONE TO TH' "ST. LOUIS BLUES" ON AN ISLAND IN TH' CHINA SEA! KNOCK ON TH' DOOR, PAT!
TRY AN' STOP ME!
2-25
HUH? WHO'S THERE?
DON'T BE ALARMED, LADY! - OUR BOAT CRACKED UP ON THE ROCKS! - WE'RE HUNGRY BUT HARMLESS!
WALK IN WITH YOUR HANDS HIGH! - IF YOU'RE LYIN' I'LL FEED YOU LEAD!
Reg. U. S. Pat. Off.: Copyright, 1936, by Chicago Tribune-N. Y. News Syndicate, Inc.
WELL, IF IT ISN'T ROBINSON CRUSOE AN' HIS MEN FRIDAY AND SATURDAY! - SAY YOUR PIECE, BOYS! - EVEN IF IT'S 'PHONEY,' I'LL BE GLAD TO HEAR SOMEBODY SPEAK ENGLISH!
MILTON CANIFF

SO YOU WERE WRECKED IN TH' STORM - YOU HEARD MY MUSIC BOX AND HERE YOU ARE! - BUT WHO ARE YOU? - WHERE DID YOU COME FROM?
2-26
WHY, WE WERE ON BOARD --- 'SMATTER PAT?
WHY - AH - WE WERE JUST OUT SAILING WHEN THE WIND PILED US UP! MY NAME IS PAT RYAN, THIS IS TERRY LEE AND OUR CHINA BOY IS CALLED CONNIE
MILTON CANIFF
I GET IT - YOU DON'T WANT TO TALK ABOUT YOURSELVES - OKAY BY ME! - BUT YOU'D BETTER HAND OVER THAT GUN! -
BUT -
Reg. U. S. Pat. Off.: Copyright, 1936, by Chicago Tribune-N. Y. News Syndicate, Inc.
I'M GLAD TO HAVE SOMEBODY TO TALK TO - BUT I WANT THE CANNONS ON MY SIDE IN CASE OF AN ARGUMENT!
YOU WIN, LADY! - HERE IT IS! - NOW THE FAMILY JEWELS ARE SAFE!

HOW ABOUT TELLING US SOMETHING OF YOURSELF - IF I'M NOT TOO BOLD...
MY NAME IS BURMA!
2-27
BURMA! - STRANGE NAME! - BUT THIS HOUSE! - AND YOU HERE ALONE - WHAT'S IT ALL ABOUT?
AH-AH! - LITTLE BOYS SHOULD BE SEEN AND NOT HEARD!
OH! - SO YOU'RE THE LADY "ON THE ROAD TO MANDALAY"! ♫ THERE'S A BURMA GIRL A-SETTIN' ♫, - ARE YOU WAITIN' FOR SOMEBODY HERE?
YES - A BLONDE GIRL ALONE ON A BARREN ISLAND IS NOT A USUAL THING!
Reg. U. S. Pat. Off.: Copyright, 1936, by Chicago Tribune-N. Y. News Syndicate, Inc.
LISTEN, GENTS - I'M GLAD TO SEE YOU, 'CAUSE I'M LONESOME! - BUT SKIP TH' QUESTIONS!
MILTON CANIFF

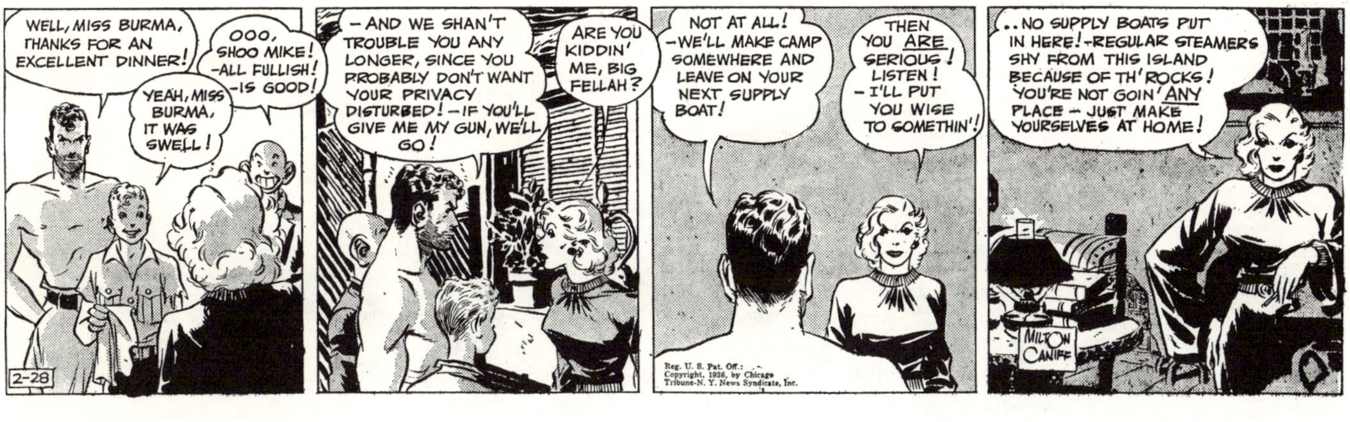
WELL, MISS BURMA, THANKS FOR AN EXCELLENT DINNER!
OOO, SHOO MIKE! -ALL FULLISH! -IS GOOD!
YEAH, MISS BURMA, IT WAS SWELL!
2-28
-AND WE SHAN'T TROUBLE YOU ANY LONGER, SINCE YOU PROBABLY DON'T WANT YOUR PRIVACY DISTURBED! -IF YOU'LL GIVE ME MY GUN, WE'LL GO!
ARE YOU KIDDIN' ME, BIG FELLAH?
NOT AT ALL! -WE'LL MAKE CAMP SOMEWHERE AND LEAVE ON YOUR NEXT SUPPLY BOAT!
THEN YOU ARE SERIOUS! LISTEN! -I'LL PUT YOU WISE TO SOMETHIN'!
Reg. U. S. Pat. Off.: Copyright, 1936, by Chicago Tribune-N. Y. News Syndicate, Inc.
..NO SUPPLY BOATS PUT IN HERE! -REGULAR STEAMERS SHY FROM THIS ISLAND BECAUSE OF TH' ROCKS! YOU'RE NOT GOIN' ANY PLACE - JUST MAKE YOURSELVES AT HOME!
MILTON CANIFF

CAN YOU BEAT IT? WE GET WRECKED ON AN ISLAND- AN' FIND A BEAUTIFUL GIRL WHO TREATS US LIKE KINGS!
POOR OL' ROBINSON CRUSOE NEVER GOT A BREAK LIKE THIS!
2-29
A SWELL FEED AND AN ELEGANT ROOM TO SLEEP IN! -THIS SEEMS LIKE SOMETHIN' OUT OF A MOVIE!
THAT BURMA GIRL PUZZLES ME! -WHY IS SHE HERE?
Reg. U. S. Pat. Off.: Copyright, 1936, by Chicago Tribune-N. Y. News Syndicate, Inc.
AW, ACT YOUR AGE, PAT! -SOMEBODY GIVES YOU A WATCH AN' YOU WANT T'SEE WHAT MAKES IT TICK! - RELAX, PAL!
MILTON CANIFF
VELLY DANGEROUS HAVE THOSE THREE PERSONS HERE, MISSY! - COME BIG TROUBLE MAYBE!
LEAVE THAT TO ME! I GOTTA HUNCH THIS DUMP ISN'T GONNA BE SO LONESOME FROM NOW ON!

PAT IS CONCERNED AT THE PRESENCE OF THE LOVELY BURMA ON A BARREN ISLAND- BUT TERRY AND CONNIE BASK IN THE WARMTH OF HER HOSPITALITY, AND DON'T BOTHER TO WORRY WHY SHE IS THERE...
3-2
Reg. U. S. Pat. Off.: Copyright, 1936, by Chicago Tribune-N. Y. News Syndicate, Inc.
UP AN' AT 'EM, PAL! - DON'T THINK YOU CAN SLEEP ALL DAY JUST 'CAUSE YOU'RE A GUEST!
OH, BOY! -IS IT SWELL TO SLEEP IN A BED AGAIN!
KNOCK ON DOOR! -IS MEBBE EVIL SPIRIT COME TO MAKE HAUNTS!
BALONEY! -OPEN IT, CONNIE!
TOP O' TH' MORNING, ME LADS! - BURMA'S COME, BEARING GIFTS!
YOUR BREAKFAST IS READY DOWNSTAIRS! -I'VE BORROWED A RAZOR AND A SHIRT FROM ONE OF MY SERVANTS FOR YOU, WONDER MAN! - SO YOU WON'T ALWAYS LOOK LIKE YOU JUST ESCAPED FROM A TRACK MEET!
MILTON CANIFF

YOU WARNED US AGAINST ASKING QUESTIONS - BUT I SURE WOULD LIKE TO KNOW HOW YOU- AND THIS HOUSE, GOT OUT ON THIS ISLAND!
AH THERE, WONDER MAN! DON'T GET INQUISITIVE AGAIN!
3-3
WHERE DO YOU GET THAT "WONDER MAN" STUFF?
WELL- I WONDER WHO YOU ARE- AN' HOW YOU GOT HERE! - I WONDER IF WE'LL EVER MEET AGAIN...
MILTON CANIFF
DON'T GIVE ME THAT! - SOUNDS LIKE SOME COLLEGE PROM TROTTER'S LINE!
WHY DID YOU ASK ME, THEN? -SHOULD I TALK LIKE THE MYSTERY WOMAN IN A PLAY?
Reg. U. S. Pat. Off.: Copyright, 1936, by Chicago Tribune-N. Y. News Syndicate, Inc.
I DON'T CARE ABOUT THAT! -BUT WHY STRING ME ALONG? YOU DON'T GIVE A HOOT ABOUT ME!
HEY! HEY! -WE'RE ARGUING ALREADY! -HAVE ANOTHER CUP O' TEA, WONDER MAN- WE'RE GONNA GET ALONG SWELL!

WHERE'S MISS BURMA?
SHE GO BY BIG ROCK! -TAKE SWIM IN OCEAN!
3-4
-SWIMMING ALONE?-THAT'S DANGEROUS BUSINESS! IF SHE GOT A CRAMP SHE'D BE HELPLESS!
MEBBE SO!
HEY, DOWN THERE!-DON'T YOU KNOW BETTER THAN TO SWIM ALONE?-YOU MIGHT DROWN!
YOUR CONCERN TOUCHES ME, WONDER MAN! -BUT DON'T WORRY...
MILTON CANIFF
... I WOULDN'T SWIM IN THIS SWELL NEW SUIT! I WAS JUST HOPING SOME ONE WOULD NOTICE THAT THE SCENERY IS NOT THE ONLY INTERESTING THING ON THIS ISLAND!
Reg. U. S. Pat. Off.: Copyright, 1936, by Chicago Tribune-N. Y. News Syndicate, Inc.

MISS BURMA, WHERE DO YOU GET THIS SWELL FOOD YOU'VE BEEN SERVING US?
THAT'S MY SECRET!-DON'T WORRY-YOU WON'T BE STUCK WITH THE CHECK!
THAT'S WHAT PUZZLES ME! SOMEBODY HAS TO PAY THE FREIGHT!
HEY, GANG! -I FOUND A SWELL RECORD! -LISTEN!
THIS LIFE'S TOO EASY!-A GOOD MEAL-TANGO MUSIC!-WE'LL BE GETTIN' FAT IF WE'RE NOT CAREFUL!
YOU MIGHT ASK THE LADY TO DANCE! -THEY SAY THAT'S GOOD EXERCISE!
SORRY, MISS BURMA! -MY SOCIAL GRACES SEEM A BIT RUSTY!
-YOU'RE GRACEFUL ENOUGH FOR ME-SOCIALLY, OR OTHERWISE! -AND WHY DON'T YOU FORGET THAT "MISS"?-MY BEST FRIENDS CALL ME "HONEY"!
MILTON CANIFF

YOU'RE A GOOD DANCER, WONDER MAN! -THE LADY IS PLEASED!
THE GENTLEMAN THANKS THE LADY-AND OBSERVES THAT SHE'S PRETTY SMOOTH HERSELF!
3-6
WOULD THE GENTLEMAN CARE TO HAVE THE LADY SING AND PLAY FOR HIM?
HE'D BE DELIGHTED!
MILTON CANIFF
♫ ♪ ....ASKED ME HOW I KNEW MY TRUE LOVE WAS TRUE-I, OF COURSE, REPLIED-WHEN YOUR HEART'S ON FIRE-SMOKE GETS IN YOUR EYES! ♫ ♪
Reg. U. S. Pat. Off.: Copyright, 1936, by Chicago Tribune-N. Y. News Syndicate, Inc.
NICE GOIN' LADY!-MIGHTY NICE!
NICE? YOU BIG LUG! -MUST YOU HAVE A TRUCK FALL ON YOU TO WAKE YOU UP? HOLY CATS!-I ALL BUT FALL ON YOUR NECK AND YOU JUST SAY IT'S NICE!

TAKE IT EASY, BURMA! -YOU'RE GETTIN' ON THE VERGE OF A DITHER!
WHY SHOULDN'T I?- I WAS SO LONELY I COULD SCREAM-THEN A BIG HANDSOME DEVIL LIKE YOU DROPS IN FROM NOWHERE...
3-7
...I'M SO CRAZY ABOUT YOU I'M GOIN' BATTY-AND YOU ACT LIKE A STORE WINDOW DUMMY!...
Reg. U. S. Pat. Off.: Copyright, 1936, by Chicago Tribune-N. Y. News Syndicate, Inc.
... I'VE HAD RAJAHS, MOVIE STARS AND JUST PLAIN MILLIONAIRES MAKE LOVE TO ME!- BUT YOU-YOU HEART BREAKIN' BEACHCOMBER -JUST STAND THERE AND GRIN!-TAKE THAT!
MILTON CANIFF
YOU KNOW, CONNIE-I ALWAYS READ THAT TH' HERO WHO PURSUES TH' BEAUTIFUL LADY TOOK AN AWFUL BEATIN' BEFORE HE WON HER!-BUT SOMETIMES I GUESS IT'S TH' GUY WHO RESISTS THAT TAKES TH' REAL DRUBBIN'!

I'VE SEEN IT IN MOVIES—BUT I NEVER THOUGHT I'D LIVE TO SEE IT IN REAL LIFE!
MISSY BURMA SHOO MIKE WRAP MOOSIC STICK 'ROUND MIST' PAT'S NOODLE!
3-9
—COUPLE O' WISE GUYS, EH?—I CAN'T EVEN GET SOCKED BY A LADY WITHOUT YOU TWO MONKEYS AROUND!
HONEST, PAT—WE WUZ JUS' WAITIN' FOR A FERRY BOAT!
—BUT SERIOUSLY, PAT—OUR GENIAL HOSTESS IS FALLIN' FOR YOU!—
SHE'S JUST LONESOME!—NOW DON'T THINK I'M JUST BEIN' MODEST!—I BELIEVE WE'RE IN A DANGEROUS SPOT—AND WE'D BETTER GET AWAY FROM HERE!
Reg. U. S. Pat. Off.: Copyright, 1936, by Chicago Tribune-N. Y. News Syndicate, Inc.
MILTON CANIFF
MAYHAP MIST' BOBBY CRUSOE LUCKY GUY AFTER ALL!—HE ONLY HAVE CANNIBALS ON HIS ISLAND!—WHEN LOVELY LADY ENTER—PEACE GO POOF!

WHERE'S MISS BURMA THIS MORNING?
SHE STAY IN ROOM!—I TRY SERVE BLEAKFAST SHE THROW CHAIR AT DOOR—SAY ME GO 'WAY!
3-10
SEEMS TO BE A HABIT OF HERS!
WHAT SAY?
Reg. U. S. Pat. Off.: Copyright, 1936, by Chicago Tribune-N. Y. News Syndicate, Inc.
—NOTHING!—LISTEN!—WE'VE GOT TO GET AWAY FROM HERE!—YOU'VE GOT TO HELP US!
IS GOOD IDEA!—GOT MOTOR BOAT IN COVE!—I TAKE YOU TO NEXT ISLAND!
—OH, SO THERE IS A BOAT HERE!—I'LL ARRANGE TO GET YOU PAID WELL FOR TAKING US OVER!
NO WANT PAY!—I TAKE YOU!—VELLY DANGEROUS YOU STAY THIS PLACE!—COME!—I FIX!
MILTON CANIFF

SNAP INTO IT, GANG!—BURMA'S SERVANT TOLD ME THERE'S A BOAT HERE!—HE'S TAKIN' US TO THE NEXT ISLAND!
AW, PAT! JUST WHEN WE'RE HAVIN' A SWELL TIME YOU WANT T' GO MEANDERIN' AWAY!
3-11
THIS SERVANT SAID IT WAS DANGEROUS TO STAY HERE—HE'S SO ANXIOUS TO GET RID OF US HE'S HAULING US FREE!—
IT MUST BE IMPORTANT OR HE'D NEVER DO SOMETHING FOR NOTHING!—OKAY—I'M READY!
Reg. U. S. Pat. Off.: Copyright, 1936, by Chicago Tribune-N. Y. News Syndicate, Inc.
MOTOR WARMIN' UP!—YOU COME SUDDEN!—WE GO BY NEXT ISLAND! IS DANGER TO DELAY!
HOLD IT!—I HEARD THAT MOTOR BOAT START AND I GUESSED YOU WERE TRYIN' TO RUN OUT ON ME!—WELL JUST FORGET IT!—NOBODY RUNS OUT ON BURMA!!
MILTON CANIFF

I'LL ATTEND TO YOU LATER FOR TRYIN' TO GET AWAY WITH MY BOAT! BEAT IT!
YES, MISSY!
3-12
DON'T BLAME YOUR SERVANT, BURMA!—IT WAS MY IDEA!—I THOUGHT IT WAS BETTER FOR US TO LEAVE—HE WAS JUST HELPING US!
THERE MUST BE A GOOD REASON WHY YOU'RE ALONE HERE!—SO WE THOUGHT IT'D BE BETTER IF WE MINDED OUR OWN BUSINESS AND LEFT!
Reg. U. S. Pat. Off.: Copyright, 1936, by Chicago Tribune-N. Y. News Syndicate, Inc.
MMM! SHE WALKED OUT ON US!—WELL, BOYS!—WE'RE GETTIN' THE OLD SILENCE TREATMENT!—WOMEN ARE NOTORIOUS TALKERS—BUT THEIR SILENCE CARRIES A THOUSAND TIMES MORE POWER!!
MILTON CANIFF

I SEE WE'RE STILL GETTIN' FED —EVEN IF THE HOSTESS IS SORE AT US! WHERE IS MISS BURMA?
SHE STAY IN ROOM! —NO TALK TO ME!— I SCARED!
3-13
DON'T WORRY! —I TOLD HER IT WAS OUR IDEA TO LEAVE HERE —YOU HAVE NOTHING TO FEAR!
IS NOT THAT!—MISSY BURMA NOT KIND TO STAY ANGLY LONG!
Reg. U. S. Pat. Off.: Copyright, 1936, by Chicago Tribune-N. Y. News Syndicate, Inc.
THEN THERE MUST BE A GOOD REASON TO MAKE YOU SHAKE THAT WAY! —TELL ME!!
I 'FRAID WHAT HAPPEN WHEN... NO! NO!— I CAN NO TELL!
THERE'S YOUR ANSWER, GANG! — WE'RE SITTIN' ON DYNAMITE — AND BURMA'S THE FUSE! — WE'VE HEARD THE RATTLE — I HOPE WE'RE AWAKE WHEN THE SNAKE STRIKES!!
MILTON CANIFF

TH' SUSPENSE OF THIS THING'S GETTIN' ME, PAT! —ALL DAY WE'VE JUST LOAFED AROUND — WAITIN'! WAITIN'!... FOR WHAT?
3-14
WISH I KNEW! BURMA STAYS IN HER ROOM— AND THE SERVANT WON'T TALK! — IT'S CREEPY BUSINESS!
ONE TIME I JUMP AT SOUND OF LI'L HOPPY TOAD!
SITTIN' AROUND MOANIN' WON'T HELP! —I'M GOIN' T' BED! —A LITTLE SHUT-EYE OUGHTA TAKE SOME KINKS OUTA MY JUMPY NERVES!
Reg. U. S. Pat. Off.: Copyright, 1936, by Chicago Tribune-N. Y. News Syndicate, Inc.
CONNIE TOO!—MEBBE HAVE BOOTIFUL DLEAM!
COMIN' PAT?
THINK I'LL HAVE ANOTHER PIPEFUL! —MIGHT GET SOME BRILLIANT IDEA FROM THE STARS! G'NIGHT, GANG!
MILTON CANIFF

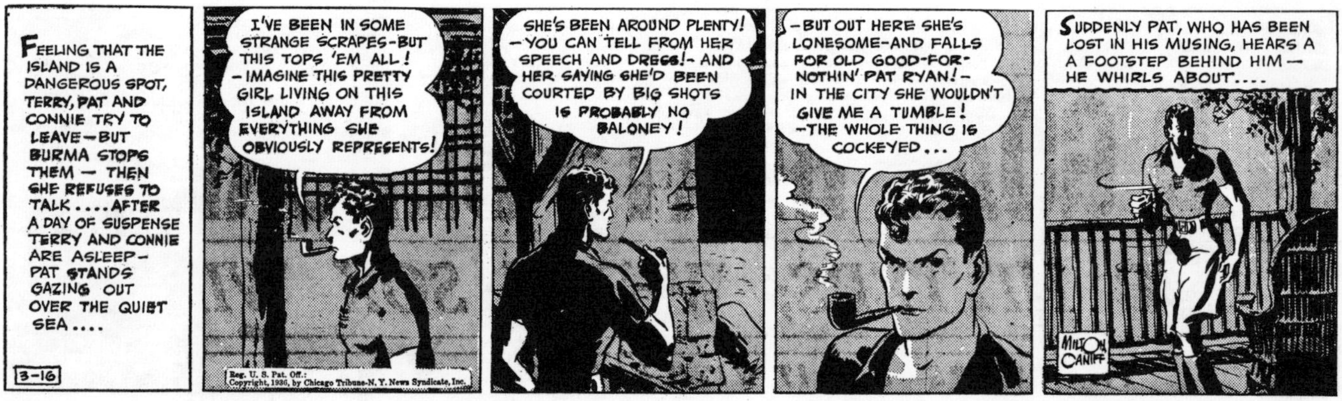
FEELING THAT THE ISLAND IS A DANGEROUS SPOT, TERRY, PAT AND CONNIE TRY TO LEAVE—BUT BURMA STOPS THEM — THEN SHE REFUSES TO TALK.... AFTER A DAY OF SUSPENSE TERRY AND CONNIE ARE ASLEEP— PAT STANDS GAZING OUT OVER THE QUIET SEA....
3-16
I'VE BEEN IN SOME STRANGE SCRAPES—BUT THIS TOPS 'EM ALL! —IMAGINE THIS PRETTY GIRL LIVING ON THIS ISLAND AWAY FROM EVERYTHING SHE OBVIOUSLY REPRESENTS!
Reg. U. S. Pat. Off.: Copyright, 1936, by Chicago Tribune-N. Y. News Syndicate, Inc.
SHE'S BEEN AROUND PLENTY! —YOU CAN TELL FROM HER SPEECH AND DRESS!—AND HER SAYING SHE'D BEEN COURTED BY BIG SHOTS IS PROBABLY NO BALONEY!
—BUT OUT HERE SHE'S LONESOME—AND FALLS FOR OLD GOOD-FOR-NOTHIN' PAT RYAN!— IN THE CITY SHE WOULDN'T GIVE ME A TUMBLE! —THE WHOLE THING IS COCKEYED...
SUDDENLY PAT, WHO HAS BEEN LOST IN HIS MUSING, HEARS A A FOOTSTEP BEHIND HIM— HE WHIRLS ABOUT....
MILTON CANIFF

HEY!— OH!—IT'S YOU!
YEAH— IT'S ME— SUCH AS I AM!
3-17
Reg. U. S. Pat. Off.: Copyright, 1936, by Chicago Tribune-N. Y. News Syndicate, Inc.
—THOUGHT YOU WERE SORE AT ME!
I WAS!
MILTON CANIFF
...MIND IF I STAND HERE?
COURSE NOT! —IT'S YOUR ISLAND! —MOONLIGHT'S FREE! GLAD TO HAVE YOU!
BRRR!— KINDA CHILLY, DON'T YOU THINK?
WHY, NO— I'M QUITE COMFORTABLE!

3-18
OH–SO YOU'RE NOT CHILLY ?
NOPE!
BEAUTIFUL NIGHT, ISN'T IT?–SORTA ROMANTIC...
YEAH, QUITE!
MILTON CANIFF
YOW! -I CAN'T STAND IT...
Reg. U. S. Pat. Off.: Copyright, 1936, by Chicago Tribune-N. Y. News Syndicate, Inc.
WH...
...WHAT'S TH MATTER WITH ME?–DO I REMIND YOU OF SOMEONE YOU DON'T LIKE!–DO I SCARE YOU? AM I POISON? IF YOU DON'T KISS ME PRETTY SOON I'M GOIN' CRAZY!

ARE YOU MADE OF STONE?–I BEG YOU TO KISS ME–AN' YOU JUST STAND THERE!
3-19
Reg. U. S. Pat. Off.: Copyright, 1936, by Chicago Tribune-N. Y. News Syndicate, Inc.
I SUPPOSE YOU FEEL PLENTY HIGH AN' MIGHTY 'CAUSE I'VE THROWN MYSELF AT YOU, LIKE A HERO WORSHIPING SCHOOL GIRL?
DON'T BE SILLY! –WHAT HAPPENS WHEN YOUR REAL BOY FRIEND SHOWS UP?
OH!–THAT'S IT! –YOU THINK I'M WAITING HERE FOR SOME GUY–AND HE'LL BEAT YOU UP WHEN HE COMES...
...YOU WANT TO MAKE LOVE TO ME–BUT YOU'RE SCARED!–I SHOULD HAVE GUESSED IT BEFORE–!–YOU'RE YELLOW!-YELLOW!
MILTON CANIFF

YELLOW? –I DON'T CARE IF EVERY MAN YOU EVER LOVED SHOWED UP HERE ARMED TO THE TEETH!
YELLOW! YELLOW!
3-20
I WAS TRYIN' TO PROTECT YOU–NOT ME! –DON'T YOU THINK I KNOW YOU'RE BEAUTIFUL?
YELLOW! YELLOW!
I'LL SHUT YOU UP! COME HERE!
OW!
Reg. U. S. Pat. Off.: Copyright, 1936, by Chicago Tribune-N. Y. News Syndicate, Inc.
MILTON CANIFF

THINK I'M YELLOW, EH?
3-21
SHUT UP!
I DIDN'T MEAN IT, PAT–HONEST I...I...
OH, DARLIN'!
HEY WHAT'S THAT?
DON'T MIND US!–WE ALWAYS LIKE TO SEE THE YOUNG FOLKS HAVE A GOOD TIME...
MILTON CANIFF
Reg. U. S. Pat. Off.: Copyright, 1936, by Chicago Tribune-N. Y. News Syndicate, Inc.

JUDAS!
HEY! WHAT'S THIS?
MILTON CANIFF
3-23
YOU WILL OBSERVE, MAGLOON, A PRIME EXAMPLE OF THE VAGARIES OF LIFE - MISS BURMA AND MR. RYAN BEING QUITE AMOROUS!
YOU KNOW HER?
YOU KNOW HIM?
Reg. U. S. Pat. Off.: Copyright, 1936, by Chicago Tribune-N. Y. News Syndicate, Inc.
OH, QUITE! - AND SINCE YOU TWO ARE SO OBVIOUSLY WELL ACQUAINTED WE CAN GET RIGHT DOWN TO BUSINESS!

WELL, YOU TRAPPED US NEATLY - I SHOULD HAVE GUESSED!..
BUT I DON'T GET IT, PAT! - I DIDN'T TRAP YOU!...
3-24
I THOUGHT YOU HAD A BOY FRIEND SOMEWHERE - BUT I NEVER DREAMED IT WOULD BE OLD WHISKERS!
BUT HE'S NOT MY BOY FRIEND - OH, PAT!
Reg. U. S. Pat. Off.: Copyright, 1936, by Chicago Tribune-N. Y. News Syndicate, Inc.
AW, WHAT'S THE DIFFERENCE! - GO INTO YOUR ACT, JUDAS - YOU'VE GOT THE FLOOR!
OH, PAT - LISTEN, WILL YOU...
MILTON CANIFF
I HAVE NO TIME FOR THESE DIME NOVEL HEROICS! - LOCK RYAN IN WITH THE TWO URCHINS!

I DON'T KNOW WHAT THIS CRAZY SET-UP IS, JUDAS - BUT YOU'D BETTER NOT HARM TERRY AND CONNIE!
3-25
THE MAN WEARIES ME! - TAKE HIM AWAY!
LEGGO, MUGG!
Reg. U. S. Pat. Off. Copyright, 1936, by Chicago Tribune-N. Y. News Syndicate, Inc.
MILTON CANIFF

OHHH BOY! - I SLEPT LIKE A LOG!
3-26
HEY CONNIE! SHAKE A LEG - LET'S SEE WHAT MISS BURMA'S GOT FOR BREAKFAST!
UMPH... GLOMP!
LAST ONE DOWNSTAIRS IS A.... HEY! FER PETE'S SAKE!!
MILTON CANIFF
Reg. U. S. Pat. Off. Copyright, 1936, by Chicago Tribune-N. Y. News Syndicate, Inc.
PAT! BLOOD! OH MY GOLLY!

PAT'S BEEN SOCKED IN TH' FACE! BRING SOME WATER!
OH HORRIBLES! EVIL DOIN'S! -CONNIE FELT IT IN BONES!
PAT! PAT! - WHAT HAPPENED? IT'S ME-TERRY!
HUH?-OH! THAT DIRTY SKUNK!-I'LL GET... WOW! MY JAW!
GET WHO? WHO HIT YOU? WHAT'S UP?-WHERE'S BURMA?
TERRIFICAL SUSPENDERS!
WAIT'LL I GET TH' BEES OUTA MY HEAD..
WELL, GANG-WE TOOK A NOSE DIVE OUT O' TH' FRYIN' PAN INTO TH' FIRE -THIS ISLAND'S A HIDEOUT FOR CAPTAIN JUDAS AND HIS PIRATES!
-WOW! AN' FIVE MINUTES AGO I WUZ FEELIN' GOOD!
3-27
MILTON CANIFF
Reg. U. S. Pat. Off.: Copyright, 1936, by Chicago Tribune-N. Y. News Syndicate, Inc.

...THEN TH' MATE CLIPPED ME WITH TH' BUTT OF HIS GUN AN' I WENT OUT COLD!
BUT PAT-HOW D'YA FIGURE THIS'S CAPTAIN JUDAS' HIDEOUT?
SIMPLE!-HE PICKS UP LOOT FROM TH' PIRATE JUNKS ON HIS TANKER-BRINGS IT HERE AND STOWS IT AWAY!
AN' BURMA'S HIS GIRL--SHE'S BEEN WAITIN' HERE FOR HIM?
SHE SAID SHE WASN'T! -BUT SEEIN'S BELIEVIN'!
AN' YOU WERE KISSIN' HER WHEN JUDAS ARRIVED?
YEAH!
A HUNDRED AN' FIFTY MILLION WOMEN IN CHINA - AN YOU WOULD BE KISSIN' HIS GIRL WHEN HE WALKED IN!
MILTON CANIFF
Reg. U. S. Pat. Off.: Copyright, 1936, by Chicago Tribune-N. Y. News Syndicate, Inc.

THE ISLAND PARADISE BECOMES A DANGEROUS SPOT WITH THE ARRIVAL OF CAPTAIN JUDAS, SKIPPER OF THE PIRATE TANKER FROM WHICH TERRY, PAT AND CONNIE HAVE RECENTLY ESCAPED...
THEY ARE LOCKED IN A ROOM IN THE HEAVILY GUARDED HOUSE....
3-30
THE ISLAND'S SWARMIN' WITH JUDAS' PIRATES! -NICE KETTLE O' MONKEY BUSINESS!
LOOK, GANG! TH' TANKER'S ANCHORED IN THAT COVE!
JUDAS MUST BE THE ONLY ONE WHO KNOWS TH' CHANNELS! -THAT'S WHY THIS PLACE IS AN IDEAL HIDEOUT FOR HIM!
THINKING IT OVER-BURMA COULDN'T HAVE TRAPPED US...
...JUDAS HAD NO WAY OF WARNING HER WE WERE AROUND-WE JUST STUMBLED IN HERE BY SHEER COINCIDENCE!
YEAH-JUS' LIKE TH' COINCIDENCE THAT CAUSED TH' TITANIC AN' THAT ICEBERG T' BE IN TH' SAME SPOT AT TH' SAME TIME!
MILTON CANIFF
Reg. U. S. Pat. Off.: Copyright, 1936, by Chicago Tribune-N. Y. News Syndicate, Inc.

THIS SUSPENSE IS GETTIN' ME GOOFY! -IS THAT GUARD STILL AT TH' DOOR?
GUESS SO! -IS LOCKED!
WISH THEY'D DO SOMETHING!
THEY WILL, SOON ENOUGH! -RELAX, SONNY BOY!
GIVE LISTEN! -IS HEAVY CLOMP-CLOMP ON STAIRWAYS! -MEBBE IS DOOM DEVILS! -GOT WOE SHIVERS AN' DUCK BUMPS!
LET 'EM COME-IF IT'S JUDAS, OR THAT MATE, I'LL GET IN ONE GOOD SOCK BEFORE THEY MOW US DOWN!
MILTON CANIFF
3-31
Reg. U. S. Pat. Off.: Copyright, 1936, by Chicago Tribune-N. Y. News Syndicate, Inc.

FOOTPRINTS IS AT PORTAL!
WHEN THEY OPEN UP, GET OUTA TH' WAY!
4-1
HOLD IT PAT—IT'S BURMA'S SERVANT!
IS SO! —WITH FOOD!
HOW'S BURMA? -WHERE'S JUDAS? -WHAT ARE THEY GONNA DO WITH US?
NO MAKE TALK!—PUT FOOD—GO SUDDEN!
Reg. U. S. Pat. Off.: Copyright, 1936, by Chicago Tribune-N. Y. News Syndicate, Inc.
NO INFORMATION -BUT WE GOT EATS! -AT LEAST JUDAS IS FEEDIN' US!
THIS ISN'T JUDAS' DOING! BURMA FIXED IT! NOTICE THE FEMININE TOUCHES?
HEY—FUNNY BUSINESS! -TEAPOT GOT RATTLE !!
MILTON CANIFF

WHAT D'YA MEAN TH' TEA POT RATTLES?
CONNIE'S GOT TH' JITTERS—HE'LL BE HEARIN' ROARS IN TH' RICE NEXT!
4-2
NO FOOLIN'S! CONNIE HEAR CLINK IN TEA POT!—STLANGE DOIN'S!
HEY!—MAYBE.. -POUR THAT TEA—QUICKLY! -SOMEONE MAY COME IN!
Reg. U. S. Pat. Off.: Copyright, 1936, by Chicago Tribune-N. Y. News Syndicate, Inc.
HURRY, CONNIE! -WHAT DO YOU FIND?
—IS MESSY TEA LEAVES IN BOTTOM OOH!—I SEE!
MILTON CANIFF
WHAT ?
A KEY!!

A KEY IN TH' TEA POT BURMA SENT US!—SHE'S ON OUR SIDE, AFTER ALL!
MAKE SOME NOISE, YOU GUYS SO TH' GUARD WON'T HEAR WHILE I TRY TH' LOCK!
4-3
FOR IT'S ALWAYS FAIR WEATHER—WHEN GOOD FELLOWS GET TOGETHER..
?
Reg. U. S. Pat. Off.: Copyright, 1936, by Chicago Tribune-N. Y. News Syndicate, Inc.
WHAT TH' DEVIL...
MILTON CANIFF
PAT! -WHAT'S WRONG!
THAT DOOR HAS AN OLD FASHIONED BOLT! -THIS KEY'S FOR A MODERN TUMBLER LOCK!

OF ALL TH' LUCK!—BURMA SMUGGLES US A KEY TO TH' DOOR—AN' IT'S TH' WRONG ONE!
—AN' SHE RISKED HER OWN NECK TO DO IT, TOO!
4-4
POOR MISSY BURMA—EVIL JUDAS MAD TO HER TOO!—WE ALL IN SAME BOAT!
Reg. U. S. Pat. Off.: Copyright, 1936, by Chicago Tribune-N. Y. News Syndicate, Inc.
BOAT! -THAT'S IT!
MILTON CANIFF
BURMA'S SERVANT ONCE TRIED TO TAKE US AWAY IN A MOTOR LAUNCH! -THIS IS TH' KEY TO THAT BOAT!

IMPRISONED IN THEIR ROOM IN BURMA'S HOUSE, TERRY, PAT AND CONNIE FIND A KEY IN THE TEA-POT SENT WITH THEIR FOOD... IT FAILS TO UNLOCK THE DOOR - BUT IT SUDDENLY OCCURS TO PAT THAT IT MAY BE THE IGNITION KEY TO BURMA'S SPEEDBOAT ..
4-6
THAT MUST BE IT, PAT! - SHE MEANS FOR US TO ESCAPE IN HER BOAT!
BUT EVIL PIRATE GENTS ARE NUMEROUS AN' NASTY! - MOST UNGOOD!
MILTON CANIFF
WE'VE GOT TO MAKE IT SOMEHOW! - IF THIS KEY'S NOT FOR THE BOAT - WELL...
DON'T SAY IT, PAL!
Reg. U S Pat Off.: Copyright, 1936, by Chicago Tribune-N. Y News Syndicate, Inc
ON THE FLOOR BELOW ANOTHER HEATED DISCUSSION IS IN PROGRESS...
JUDAS, I'VE TOLD YOU THOSE BOYS JUST HAPPENED TO LAND HERE!!
OBVIOUSLY IT IS SHEER COINCIDENCE... BUT THAT DOES NOT ALTER THE FACT....
...THAT THEY NOT ONLY DISABLED THE TANKER - BUT THEY KNOW TOO MUCH! - NO ONE KNOWS THEY ARE HERE - SO NO ONE WOULD MISS THEM IF THEY WERE QUIETLY... SHALL WE SAY - ELIMINATED?

YOU MEAN YOU'D KILL THOSE THREE SWELL GUYS?
FROM WHAT WE SAW EARLIER, I SHOULD GUESS YOUR MAIN CONCERN IS WITH THE RYAN CHAP!
4-7
ALL RIGHT - HE WAS KISSING ME - WHAT BUSINESS IS THAT OF YOURS?
ALTHOUGH OURS HAS ALWAYS BEEN A BUSINESS RELATIONSHIP, YOU MUST BE AWARE THAT I AM IN LOVE WITH YOU!!
MILTON CANIFF
YOU? - DON'T MAKE ME LAUGH - YOU'RE IN LOVE WITH YOURSELF AND YOUR MONEY...
Reg. U. S. Pat. Off.: Copyright, 1936, by Chicago Tribune-N. Y. News Syndicate, Inc.
... AND BESIDES I COULDN'T LOVE YOU, YOU DREAMY-EYED SHRIMP! - IN FACT, I HATE YOU - AND I HOPE YOU CHOKE ON ONE OF THOSE BIG WORDS YOU USE!!

WITHOUT ME, YOU'D BE A NAVIGATION OFFICER ON SOME RUSTY, TWO-BIT FREIGHTER!
I MIGHT REMIND YOU THAT WITHOUT ME - YOU WOULD BE GRACING SOME SINGAPORE GUTTER!
4-8
Reg. U S. Pat. Off.: Copyright, 1936, by Chicago Tribune-N. Y News Syndicate, Inc.
JUST BECAUSE I WAS BROKE WHEN I MET YOU DOESN'T MEAN I HAVEN'T HAD PLENTY!
IT SEEMS OUR OTHERWISE PLEASANT ASSOCIATION HAS BEEN DISRUPTED BY THIS MAN RYAN!
WHAT'S THAT TO YOU? - IF I GO FOR HIM, IT'S NONE OF YOUR BUSINESS!
PERHAPS SO...
... AND SINCE YOU ARE SO FOND OF HIM IT MIGHT BE WELL IF I JUST ELIMINATED YOU, TOO!!
MILTON CANIFF

SO! YOU CAN'T HAVE ME - AND YOU WANT TO KILL ME SO NO ONE ELSE CAN?
PRECISELY!
4-9
Reg U S. Pat. Off.: Copyright, 1936, by Chicago Tribune-N. Y. News Syndicate, Inc.
AND JUST HOW DO YOU INTEND TO KILL ME?
A SINGLE BULLET IN YOUR BRAIN WOULD DO IT! - YOU WOULD FEEL NO PAIN - THERE WOULD BE LITTLE BLOOD...
... YOU WOULD BE AS EXQUISITE IN DEATH AS YOU ARE IN LIFE...
I ALWAYS THOUGHT YOU WERE A LITTLE BATTY - NOW I KNOW IT...
MILTON CANIFF
... BUT YOU WILL BE INTERESTED TO KNOW THAT I HAVE A FULL STATEMENT ABOUT YOU IN A SAFE DEPOSIT BOX IN SINGAPORE! IF THE BANK DOESN'T HEAR FROM ME ONCE A MONTH THEY HAVE ORDERS TO OPEN THAT BOX!!

YOU HAVE PAPERS IN YOUR SAFE DEPOSIT BOX WHICH TELL OF MY CRIMES! - BUT IF I AM IN THE UNITED STATES WHEN THE BOX IS OPENED I WILL BE SAFE!
DON'T LOOK AT ME THAT WAY, JUDAS!
4-10
.. IT WOULD BE A MONTH BEFORE THE POLICE STARTED SEARCHING...
MEANWHILE, YOU WILL NOT BE CONCERNED - AH, NO, MY SWEET - YOU WILL BE DEAD!!
MILTON CANIFF

PAT - IT'S DARK NOW! - WE'VE GOT TO BUST OUTA HERE TONIGHT!
AN' THIS KEY'S GOT TO FIT BURMA'S BOAT OR WE'RE SUNK!
MILTON CANIFF
4-11
REMEMBER, WE CALL THE GUARD AND YOU'RE HANGING FROM TH' RAFTERS READY TO DROP ON HIM...
HEY! DID YOU HEAR A SCREAM?
I HEAR! - SOUND LIKE MISSY BURMA!
GEE! WHAT D'YA S'PPOSE...?
LOOK! - SMOKE!
TH' JOINT'S ON FIRE!

HEARING A SCREAM FROM BELOW THEIR LOCKED ROOM, TERRY, PAT AND CONNIE PAUSE IN THEIR PLANS TO ESCAPE - THEN, THROUGH THE CRACKS IN THE FLOOR COMES SMOKE!
4-13
IS FIRE! - OOH! MEBBE WE GET SIZZLED LIKE BACON!
LISTEN! - GUYS YELLIN' OUTSIDE!
TH' CREW FROM TH' TANKER IS RUNNIN' THIS WAY!
SMOKE GETS LIKE FOG! - IS TICKLE NOSE!
NOW'S OUR CHANCE! - WE CAN MAKE A ROPE - DROP OUT TH' WINDOW AN' HEAD FOR BURMA'S BOAT!
THAT SCREAM WE HEARD MEANS SHE'S IN TROUBLE! - I'M GOIN' DOWNSTAIRS AND FIND OUT!
MILTON CANIFF

PAT! - YOU CAN'T GO DOWNSTAIRS! THIS PLACE IS A FURNACE! LET'S BUST OUT TH' WINDOW!
4-14
BURMA'S DONE RIGHT BY US! - IF SHE'S IN TROUBLE WE OWE IT TO HER TO LEND A HAND! - YOU HEAD FOR THE BOAT - I'LL JOIN YOU!
YOU CAN'T PAT!
LISTEN! - TH' FLAMES ARE CRACKLIN' OUTSIDE TH' DOOR! - YOU'D NEVER LIVE IN THAT FIRE!
MILTON CANIFF
EVEN IF JUDAS IS MAD AT BURMA HE'D NEVER LET HER BURN UP! - TH' PIRATES'LL RESCUE HER! - LET'S BEAT IT WHILE WE CAN!
YOU WIN, PAL! LET'S GO!

4-15
TH TANKER CREW'S AROUND FRONT FIGHTIN' TH' FIRE! — IF WE RUN FOR TH' DOCK THEY MAY NOT SEE US!
MILTON CANIFF
DOWN THE PATH BEHIND THE HUTS! — LOOKS AS IF WE'RE GONNA WIN!...
SINK ME! — WOT'S THIS?
Reg. U. S. Pat. Off.: Copyright, 1936, by Chicago Tribune-N. Y. News Syndicate, Inc.

4-16
IT'S THEM PRISONERS! DON'T LET 'EM RUN OUT AGAIN!
GET THAT MOTOR WARMED! — I'LL HOLD 'EM OFF!
SLICE 'IM DOWN, LADS! HE'S ASKIN' FOR IT!
Reg. U. S. Pat. Off.: Copyright, 1936, by Chicago Tribune-N. Y. News Syndicate, Inc.
I'VE BEEN WAITIN' FOR THIS CHANCE!
MILTON CANIFF

4-17
TH' IGNITION KEY FITS! — SHE'S CHUGGIN', PAT! — COME ON!
THERE'S SOMETHIN' TO REMEMBER ME BY!
GIVE 'ER TH' GUN, BOYS! — AN' MAKE ROOM FOR PAPA!
MILTON CANIFF
Reg. U. S. Pat. Off.: Copyright, 1936, by Chicago Tribune-N. Y. News Syndicate, Inc.

4-18
RUN, PAT! THEY'RE RIGHT BEHIND YOU!
Reg. U. S. Pat. Off.: Copyright, 1936, by Chicago Tribune-N. Y. News Syndicate, Inc.
NO TIME TO CAST OFF! STEP ON IT!
MILTON CANIFF

JUDAS' FIRST MATE AND TWO SAILORS PLUNGE INTO THE OCEAN AS THE POWERFUL MOTOR BOAT PULLS THE FLIMSY DOCK FROM ITS MOORINGS!...
4-20
CUT THAT ROPE, CONNIE! – WE'RE DRAGGIN' LUMBER ENOUGH TO BUILD A SCHOONER!
IS DONE!
WOW! THAT WAS CLOSE!
LOOK! – HOUSE BURN LIKE BOOTIFUL FIREWORKS!
MILTON CANIFF
– AN' WE JUST MIGHT HAVE BEEN INSIDE! BOY! – WE'RE LUCKY!
YEAH – AND WE'LL NEED MORE LUCK TO GET US TO THE MAINLAND! DON'T GET HUNGRY – WE'RE EATING FOOD FOR THOUGHT FOR AWHILE!
Reg. U. S. Pat. Off.: Copyright, 1936, by Chicago Tribune-N. Y. News Syndicate, Inc.

WHEN THE SUN'S UP WE CAN HEAD DUE WEST AND STRIKE MAINLAND!
IF OUR GAS HOLDS!
THEN WHAT?
HARD TO SAY! – IF WE STRIKE A TOWN IT'LL BE SWELL – IF NOT... WELL... IT'S JUNGLE OR NOTHING!
Reg. U. S. Pat. Off.: Copyright, 1936, by Chicago Tribune-N. Y. News Syndicate, Inc.
YOU'RE TIRED, TERRY – CRAWL IN THAT CABIN AND CATCH SOME SLEEP!
GOLLY, I AM! – GUESS IT'S LETDOWN FROM ALL THE EXCITEMENT!
PAT! LOOK!
MILTON CANIFF

WHAT'S WRONG, TERRY?
JIMMINY! LOOK!
4-22
BURMA!
MILTON CANIFF
IS SHE HURT... OR SUMTHIN'?
SHE'S OUT COLD! – THERE'S A BUMP ON HER HEAD! – BRING SOME WATER!
BURMA! CAN YOU HEAR ME? IT'S PAT!
DON'T LOOK AT ME THAT WAY, JUDAS! ... WHAT IF I WAS KISSING PAT.....
Reg. U. S. Pat. Off.: Copyright, 1936, by Chicago Tribune-N. Y. News Syndicate, Inc.

I DON'T WANT TO DIE!... I'M TOO PRETTY TO DIE! ... JUDAS, YOU'RE CRAZY, I TELL YOU...
BURMA! WAKE UP! – YOU'RE SAFE! – DON'T YOU KNOW ME?
4-23
HUH....? – WHERE AM I?
YOU'RE ON YOUR OWN BOAT – AND JUDAS IS FAR AWAY! – IT'S ME, PAT!
Reg. U. S. Pat. Off.: Copyright, 1936, by Chicago Tribune-N. Y. News Syndicate, Inc.
PAT!... – OH BOY, I NEVER WAS SO GLAD TO SEE ANYBODY IN ALL MY LIFE!!
LOOKEE! LOOKEE! – COMES SHORE IN DISTANCE! HOTSY DANDY!
MILTON CANIFF

MAKE FOR THAT INLET, CONNIE! IT'S FAIRLY SHELTERED!
IS JUST IN TIME! - GAS 'MOST ALL CHUGGED UP!
4-24
Reg. U. S. Pat. Off.: Copyright, 1936, by Chicago Tribune-N. Y. News Syndicate, Inc.
SIT DOWN UNDER THESE TREES, BURMA! - WE'LL TRY AND FIND SOME FRESH WATER!
GEE, MISS BURMA - HOW'D YOU GET IN TH' BOAT?
WELL, JUDAS AND I HAD AN ARGUMENT - I THREW A LAMP AT HIM - THAT'S WHAT STARTED THE FIRE! - I SCREAMED AND RUSHED TOWARD THE DOCK...
...I KNEW YOU'D BREAK OUT IN THE EXCITEMENT AND USE THE BOAT TO ESCAPE - I MUST HAVE STUMBLED AND KNOCKED MYSELF OUT AS I ENTERED THE CABIN WITH MY BAG...
OH!... WHERE'S THAT BAG! OH!
MILTON CANIFF

THE BAG I CARRIED ON THE BOAT! - IT SHOULD BE IN THE CABIN! - I MUST HAVE IT!
SHOO MIKE! CONNIE KETCHUM!
4-25
OH, THANKS, CONNIE! - I WAS SCARED STIFF FOR A MINUTE!
YOU MEAN YOU STOPPED TO PACK A BAG AFTER THROWING A LAMP AT JUDAS...?
Reg. U. S. Pat. Off.: Copyright, 1936, by Chicago Tribune-N. Y. News Syndicate, Inc.
MILTON CANIFF
WELL, YOU'RE LUCKY TO HAVE SOME CLOTHES - YOU'LL NEED 'EM!...
CLOTHES, NOTHING...
...THIS BAG CONTAINS ALL THE JEWELRY JUDAS PIRATED FROM VARIOUS STEAMERS! - IT'S WORTH ABOUT A QUARTER OF A MILLION DOLLARS!

ESCAPING FROM JUDAS AND HIS MEN IN BURMA'S SPEED BOAT, TERRY, PAT AND CONNIE ARE SURPRISED TO FIND BURMA ON BOARD... THEY ARE MORE AMAZED WHEN THEY LEARN THE BAG SHE CARRIES CONTAINS A QUARTER MILLION DOLLARS IN STOLEN JEWELRY...
4-27
YOU MEAN YOU HAVE ALL THE JEWELS JUDAS PIRATED FROM VARIOUS STEAMERS?
SURE! WANTA SEE?
Reg. U. S. Pat. Off.: Copyright, 1936, by Chicago Tribune-N. Y. News Syndicate, Inc.
NECKLACES! BRACELETS! EARRINGS!
BROOCHES! BAR PINS! PENDANTS!
IT'S A FEAST FOR THE EYES, EH, BOYS?
EYES NO NEED FEAST!..
MILTON CANIFF
...BUT TUMMY WOULD TRADE WHOLE PILE OF SPARKLES FOR JUICY MELICAN HAMBURGER!

SO YOU HIJACKED THIS JEWELRY FROM OLD JUDAS AFTER YOU SOCKED HIM WITH A LAMP?
HIJACKED NOTHING...
4-28
...I HAD THIS COMING TO ME! ..SAY... I DON'T BELIEVE YOU REALLY KNOW WHAT I AM - DO YOU?
I'M BEGINNING TO GUESS...
SUPPOSE YOU TELL ME, IF YOU'RE SO SMART!
YOU WERE THE FENCE FOR JUDAS' PIRATES! - HE'D HOLD UP SHIPS - YOU'D WAIT ON THAT ISLAND... TAKE THE JEWELS TO SOME DISTANT CITY AND POSE AS SOME GRAND DUCHESS..
MILTON CANIFF
Reg. U. S. Pat. Off.: Copyright, 1936, by Chicago Tribune-N. Y. News Syndicate, Inc.
...YOU'D TELL THE LOCAL BOYS YOU WERE BROKE AND HAD TO SELL THE CROWN JEWELS.. THEY'D SWALLOW IT, AND PAY YOU WELL FOR THE STOLEN STUFF... AM I RIGHT?
YOU'RE RIGHT - AND I'M AMAZED!

ABOUT THE AUTHOR: Milton Caniff is one of the greatest figures in the history of American Comics. He is often referred to as the "Rembrandt of the comics". Caniff has been a popular as well as critical success. He has had one active newpaper strip or another appearing almost continously for over 50 years. In the early 1930's Caniff produced **DICKIE DARE.** In 1934 he began **TERRY & THE PIRATES** which he continued until 1946. In 1947 Caniff introduced **STEVE CANYON** which still appears today in newspapers across America.

OTHER CANIFF BOOKS FROM NBM

TERRY & THE PIRATES COLLECTORS EDITION

These hardbound, gold stamped books reprint the complete TERRY & THE PIRATES. Every daily and Sunday strip (including never before reprinted Sundays from 1934 and 1935) is printed in full size. 8 volumes of this 12 volume series have been printed. The series is scheduled for completion in 1987. Write for more information on availability and prices.

MILTON CANIFF - REMBRANDT OF THE COMIC STRIP

The original version of this book appeared in 1946 as Caniff was finishing his work on TERRY & THE PIRATES. Comic historian Rick Marschall has updated this 1980 edition. There are many beautiful rare illustrations and blowups of Caniff's art.

Paperback – $6.95   Collectors Edition (Hardcover) – $13.50

WELCOME TO CHINA

Vol. 1 of this paperback TERRY Series is available at $5.95. Vol. 1 starts with the very first daily strip, and the finale is a cliff hanging battle of wits on a desert island. 64 pp, color cover.

All orders:

NBM PUBLISHING CO.
156 E. 39TH ST.
NEW YORK, NY 10016
add $2.00 p&h per book

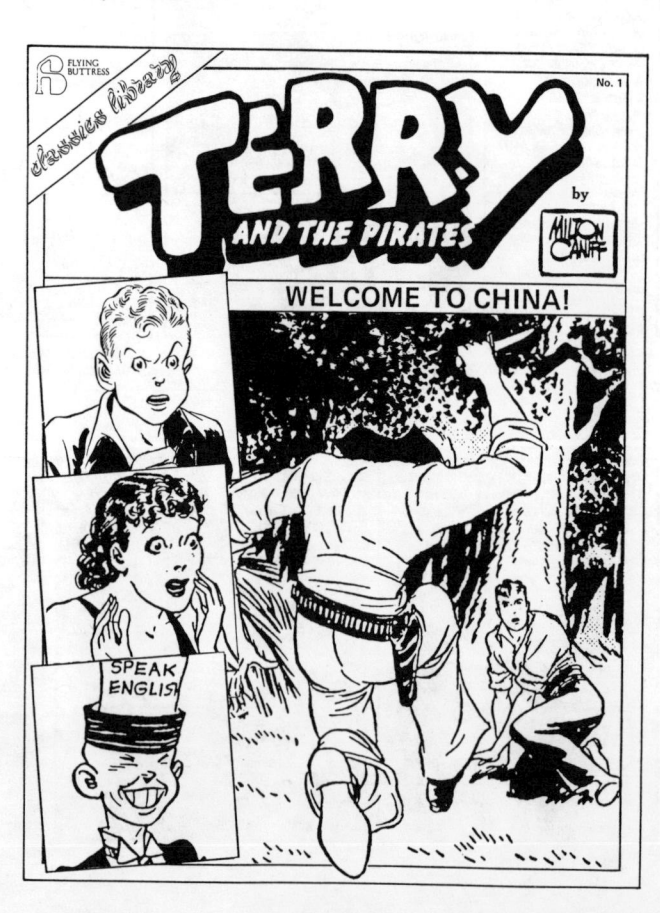